How Algebra Split the December Night

Nina Olsson

Grosvenor House
Publishing Limited

This book is published by
Grosvenor House Publishing Ltd
Link House
140 The Broadway, Tolworth, Surrey, KT6 7HT.
www.grosvenorhousepublishing.co.uk

A CIP record for this book
is available from the British Library

ISBN 978-1-83975-455-5

This book is dedicated to all lost souls,
may you be lost no more.

Always follow your dreams.

Contents

Part Three – Life in a New Age

Part One
"Revelations"

Chapter One

Aunty A – Aninya

Who would give their child a name like Algebra? Well, my parents did. Of course, it made me different from birth, not that I really minded, nothing wrong with being different, although I often pondered on the why. My parents disappeared when I was very young, barely 3, so I could not ask them. From what I had learnt, they were not remotely interested in mathematics or anything connected with it. In that assumption, however, I was very wrong. It would remain a mystery for a long time.

I convinced myself that it was some sort of code, perhaps I was a "sleeper" for some foreign power, or more likely, that my parents were just mad.

I lived with my Aunt Aninya on the edge of the town, in a small cottage filled with the most amazing things. I had never seen anything like them anywhere else. My friends' parents had nothing like them, not that I had many friends.

Aunty A, as I called her, told me stories every night, but never really about my parents, even though I asked every time. I supposed that I could not have come here by all by myself, could I?

Her stories were always set in some strange place, but my favourites were the ones set in the forests of Siberia, which as I grew older I realised was where we lived.

We lived in a small village surrounded by a large lake, where mystical creatures lived. The lake was so deep that no one had ever found the bottom of it. The fishermen would not go out at night because if they did they never came back, at least not looking like themselves. Perhaps that's where my parents went, I thought.

One night, while talking around the crackling fire, she, Aunty A that is, told me she had a bracelet for me. It was strange-looking, with lots of different charms around it in the form of little coloured animal shapes. She said it was for the future, to fulfil my destiny, whatever that was.

Another fisherman had gone missing the night before. Aunty A knew him well, they had grown up together. It was very strange, all the comings and goings. There were new arrivals too, strangers arriving in the village but sounding as if they knew the place. It was all very odd.

My days continued as normal, well, as normal as it could be for me. I foraged for food at first light, spent some hours at the small school, where, as always, my name would cause gales of laughter, and then later Aunty A and I would walk down to the harbour to see who was there.

It carried on like this until I was 14. One of the fishermen, Lukas, had a son called Tomas, a year older than me. He always seemed pleased to see me. We would talk for hours on the days that his father would be ashore, mending the nets. I loved spending time with Tomas. Though only a little older than me, he seemed to know so much. Sometimes he would go out on the boat with his father, but much of the time he spent repairing the nets and getting the catch ready for sale. We would sit on the pebbled shore, talking and staring out at the lake or the river behind us.

He told me about the mountains that surrounded the lake and of the many animals that roamed the upland areas. There were bears, foxes, many species of deer, and even red squirrels. I had never seen any of these creatures, only on my little bracelet, and I marvelled at how much he knew. He said it was because he spent his time with the older fishermen who had lived their lives around the lake. He also said that was why it was not safe to wander about at night, not that I wanted to, as this was my time for Aunty A's stories.

Our lake, my knowledgeable friend told me, was a freshwater type, which was so large it looked like the sea. He was right, you could see to the horizon. Seals could be seen on occasion, bobbing their heads up and down as they fished the waters for their food. They did not affect the fishermen as the fish were plentiful, the main ones being omul, a type of white fish. These were the ones that were caught and sold at the markets surrounding the lake. I loved all of the activity when the boats came in, and had watched them since I was a child.

Aunty A would take me once a month to buy our supplies, and I enjoyed meeting with the other lake folk, this was my happy and settled life. The chatter of the people and the screeching of the Mongolian gulls overhead was the music that I knew and loved. I had met Tomas on one of our trips to market and discovered, to my joy, that he lived in the same village, Listvenichnoye. He became my friend, really the only one I had.

Every winter the lake would freeze over and we would take our sleds and play on the ice. We could not stay out too long because the wind chill would make the temperature so low there was a danger of frostbite. There were stories of soldiers who had tried to cross the lake one winter and who had died there because of the extreme cold. We were told from a young age to stay near the edges and only play for a short time.

Nearby, a new railway line had been built, that stretched for many many miles, part of it connecting our village with the town of Irkutsk, where my father had worked, in the large factory. We heard that this railway could also take you to the capital city of Moscova, wherever that was. It sounded very exciting. Tomas and I talked of going there one day, and I wondered if that was where my parents had gone. I tried to talk with Aunty A about it, but she just said that I would find out everything when it was the proper time. I wanted the proper time to be now, I was nearly 15 and impatient to know everything there was to know about family and boys. My feelings for Tomas had deepened and I did not know how to deal with them.

One day, Aunty A told me I was to leave. She had written a letter to an aunt who lived in Moscova and was awaiting a reply. I did not want to leave, this was all I knew. She did not explain why. I was very upset but there was no changing her mind. I asked again about my parents, but was given no answer. I really could not understand it. I was sorry to say goodbye to Tomas, but Aunty A said it would be for the best. For whom? I wondered.

The dreaded letter came, and so we left.

Chapter Two

Aunty E – Elena

I was to travel to Moscova, the capital city for the region, the place that Tomas and I wondered about, to stay with another aunty, Elena, whom I had never heard of before. I wondered if she would know about my parents.

Aunty A took me to the train station, and to my seat in a compartment with another family. There were six of us in a small space, but this was a comfort to me, travelling alone at 14 years old. I thought about telling them my name was Tasha, but Aunty A spoiled the idea by introducing me to the other people. Of course, we then had to go through the usual laughs and questions.

The other family was a mother, father and three children – two girls and a boy. I supposed the boy was about my age, the two girls younger. They seemed to be nice and Aunty A seemed to know them, but then she knew many people.

The journey took three days, over which time we got to know each other more. The two girls, Katrina and Olga, were I thought about 10 and 12 years old, and quite silly little creatures. The boy was 16 and his name was Petyr.

I had been given lots of food for the journey, which I shared with them, as was the custom on the long haul trains. The days were good, staring out of the windows at the birch tree forests, rivers and small towns we could see near the train tracks. There was lots going on – the track maintenance crews, the children walking to school, the old ladies in their head coverings, appearing like ghosts out of the forests, going to market.

The nights were not so good, the train creaked noisily along the rails, rolling from side to side. It was difficult to sleep sitting upright in the seat, and the two girls talked and laughed half the night. Petyr and his parents did not seem to notice and slept soundly. I wished that I could too.

One compensation was looking out at the night sky and the stars so close and so bright. I was sure that if I could lean out of the train I would be able to touch them. Sadly I could not do that, it would have been far too dangerous.

The three days went by and soon I was in the city. Aunty Elena was there to meet me. They were very strange, my aunties. Aunty E, as I now call her, was not like her sister at all. Whereas Aunty A was mysterious and would tell me wondrous stories, Aunty E was very business-like. I suppose that's what came of living in a big city.

There was one very odd thing about Aunty E, she lived underground in a cave-like space, reached through a series of tunnels. At the entrance was a big steel gate that clanged shut when she did not want to see anyone.

Having come from the countryside, I did not like it, being closed in, but at least I felt safe there.

I had my 15th birthday, so I did not have to go to school anymore, which I was happy about, except I didn't get to see any other people and began to feel like a prisoner.

Occasionally we would go out to get food supplies, and I was surprised that, like Aunty A, she knew a lot of people. So, I reasoned, that she must come out into the air on many occasions. Was it just me she wanted to keep hidden? Was this all to do with my parents?

One day we went into the heart of the city. It was like a fortress, a huge wall surrounded a palace and other buildings that I was informed were churches with tombs containing famous people from the past. Now this was much more interesting. I wanted to go and see, but was hurried across a large cobbled square and into a large building to buy our supplies. It had lots of sections selling goods, and at its centre was a beautiful large fountain – a great place for meeting people and eating ices. Before we left, she took me to the beautiful Alexander Gardens, with its many rows of vibrant flowers, fairy tale figures and the fountain with four mighty horses rearing up out of the spray. I had never seen anything like it. It was magnificent. The sight of it made up for all of the long days staring at the walls of our underground home.

I could hear many different accents, some of which I recognised from home. I wanted to go and talk to them, but Aunty E said I must not, which of course made me all the more determined to do so.

Another time we went down to the canal, to a small park there. We saw many couples, some brides still in their beautiful dresses, posing for their portraits. I loved to watch the artists at work, painting the happy faces of the men and women on their special day. I wondered if I would ever get married, but doubted it as I was never allowed to go out on my own. I thought of Tomas from my village and how I missed him and our talks on the lakeshore.

On another outing we went into a large square building. It looked pretty on the outside, but once inside it had an ominous, heavy feeling. I did not like it. I was about to ask some questions but one look at Aunty E's face told me to keep quiet. Was there some connection with my parents here? She did not introduce me to anyone so I knew that whatever it was about, it must be serious. I was relieved to be out of there. Our journey home was spent in silence.

I had thought that Aunty A was difficult to be with, but Aunty E was much worse. I suppose I was afraid of her, although she could be really caring on occasion. Aunty A was my mother's sister and Aunty E, I learnt, was from my father's family. I had thought that they were sisters, but they were not. I so much wanted to know about my parents, so instead of any real information, I made up fantastical stories about them and their adventures. Not that I told anyone, they were just for me, a little world to escape into when the real one became too hard to bear.

Aunty E did care for me, in her way, but me being an inquisitive young woman, I wanted to get out and join with the rest of humanity going about their lives outside of this underground space.

I had always supposed that it was just us who lived here, but one day, while exploring, I found a door and behind it were other families. I was so pleased to meet with other people. This time I said I was Tasha, so no one knew any different. I kept these friends a secret and went to see them whenever I could. It seemed to me that every time I made any friends, I had to move away. I was very quiet about these new people and made them promise that if they ever met Aunty E they were to say nothing of my visits.

One evening we went on a boat ride down the river which I really enjoyed. When we were back at home relaxing, we started to have a good talk. I decided to take the chance and mention my parents. At first she did not say anything, but as the evening wore on she started to talk about my father, Sergei, and how when they were teenagers they had moved from their village to the lake where they met my mother's family. They vaguely knew each other. My mother's younger sister Ekaterina, known to everyone as Katya, was the sister everyone remembered most. She was a bright-eyed, adventurous child. She now lived in Romania. She had run off to be with the travelling fair people. My grandmother had never forgiven her.

I listened carefully to everything she told me, but at the end of it I still had no idea of what had happened to my parents or how I had come to be given a name like Algebra. I decided the best way was to learn a little more each time we spoke, without appearing to be too inquisitive. I was now 16, but as I was too young to work, days were spent around our cave-like home.

I did like my Aunty E, but was very happy when I had time to myself. I invented a whole new world where I would go and have many exciting adventures. Sometimes Tomas would be there, with his calm fisherman's face, deeply tanned from being in the open air on the lakeside. Sometimes my new friend from the train, Petyr, was with me, with his two laughing sisters. Sometimes it would be the people from behind the secret door.

One day, after one of my visits, Aunty E saw me coming back, and from the look on her face I knew two things. One, that she was very angry, and two, that I would be forced to move on. I was right, plans were very quickly put into place for me to stay with Aunty Katya in Romania. I had no time to say goodbye to my friends, which made me sad. After a long journey, we reached the village of aunt number three. She was extremely surprised to see us there so quickly but made us very welcome.

I was pleased to see that we were at least above ground, and I liked Aunty K immediately. She was younger and full of life, smiling all of the time. Aunty E stayed a few days then went back to her city. I wanted to ask so many questions, but I realised that I would have to be patient if I was to get any answers. Better to concentrate on day-to-day living, at least at first.

Chapter Three

Aunty K – Ekaterina (Katya)

Aunty K took me out with her around the town. I even got to speak with some people, but of course they knew nothing of me or my parents. I began to wonder if I really had parents, and had not just arrived fully formed with Aunty A. No, that was ridiculous, but I did wonder.

I thought that somewhere there must be some pictures, so one day when I was alone I decided to look for them. Aunty K was much more easy-going than my other aunts so I thought that she would be the most likely to have some evidence of my parents' existence. At the same time, I idly wondered why there were no uncles.

Aunty K's house had lots of intriguing items. I thought that it must have been so exciting, living in a caravan, moving from town to town, setting up the fair, seeing all the happy faces as they came to enjoy all that was on offer. I thought that I would have liked to have done that too. It took me quite some time to find some pictures, I had to be careful as I did not want her to know that I had been prying into her private things, but I so desperately wanted to find some information. I had thought of nothing else for as long as I could remember.

At last I came across a small painting of a lady who looked very much like me. She had dark hair and sparkling brown eyes. Although mine were blue, I was sure she was my mother. Standing next to her was a young man with golden hair and light eyes, that I was convinced were of the brightest blue. These people had to be my parents.

I stared and stared at it, trying very hard to see any details that would tell me where it was, but sadly there was nothing definite. It could have been anywhere, but in my heart I believed it to be Siberia. I carefully put everything back and sat to await the return of Aunty K.

I could not get the painting out of my mind and really wanted to ask about it, but knew I must not as Aunty K would know I had been through her things and that I had broken her trust. One evening we had been sitting in her small garden after our meal, watching the sky change into its golden cloak as the sun slowly sank into the hills, when she suddenly announced that I was to have some work.

Being now nearly 17, she decided that I could be trusted on my own out in the wider world. I was thrilled, I had felt like a prisoner for most of my life and now I would have some freedom. Of course, I wasn't to be entirely free as the work was with some friends of hers, but at least it was out of the house and I was going to meet other people.

The next morning I put on my best clothes and went with Aunty K to a part of the town I did not know. The main square had large buildings on all sides and in the middle a beautiful fountain that looked like a cake with many tiers. She told me that once the sun set there were lanterns that made the dark waters shine with different colours. Now *that* I really would like to see, I thought.

I was taken to work by my aunt and met her each evening for the walk back home. As it was still summer, it was not yet dark enough to see the beautiful fountain lit up. Maybe in the shorter days of the winter I would see it in all its glory. I was told very firmly that I must not mention my parents to anyone. My name had now been changed to Anna, similar to Aunty A back in my home village. I suppose that my real name, Algebra, would have prompted too many questions.

I had agreed to everything because it was wonderful to be out and to have some time of my own. The job was not too bad, I was to be a filing clerk in a shipping firm, along with 10 other young people and a very stern older person in charge. Once introduced and shown our duties, we were to work in silence until our lunch break. The room had a large urn containing the hot water that we used to make our drinks. The noise in that room was very loud, all of us being suddenly released from our working silence. It reminded me of the screeching of the flocks of birds that visited the lake shoreline, and in a strange way made me feel very homesick.

Two of the girls came to talk to me, they were local but had parents who were Russian. We became friends and when we wanted to talk about something private we would revert to a form of Russian that we could all understand. Aunty K and I started to get more friendly and she had taught me some Romanian. The rest of the workers were local, mostly from villages near to the town. The town was called Brasov, not very big, but a nice place with boulevards, a large square, and a big church that had been in a fire years before, which had charred it on the outside. No one seemed to know its real name, it was just known as the Black Church.

I wondered how the two girls knew of my background, but did not give it too much thought, I was just happy that I had some new friends. The work was not too hard and soon I was looking forward to going there each day. Eventually, Aunty K agreed to let me travel on my own, although she still came down to the tram stop to see me off and to meet me at the end of the day. If ever I was a little late, she would be worried and cross if I could not give her a good reason why.

In my work, I was tasked with creating inventories for goods being exported to other countries. Some had exotic names like France, Germany and Wallonia. I was intrigued, and I wondered if my parents were in any of them. Of course, I did not discuss it with anyone, not even Aunty K.

I started to get more friendly with the two girls at work and we would spend our lunch breaks together. The older of the two was Natalya and she had come to Romania when she was 5 years old, her parents having left the Crimea area during the war years. I suppose she must have been about 19 or even 20 when I met her. The other girl, Yana, was my age and much quieter. At first I thought she was a "little grey mouse", but once I got to know her I realised that she was very interesting and had lots of stories to tell. She had been born in Brasov but brought up in a Russian-speaking household. I desperately wanted to tell her my story, but Aunty K had told me to be very careful about speaking to anyone, especially as a whole new life had been invented for me, as well as my new name.

The days went by quickly and I found that I really enjoyed my work and the people that I met there. The rest of the workers were of different ages, but still young I would say. Natalya seemed to be the office leader, for our little section at least. She had many talks with the manager behind closed doors. We supposed it was about schedules and things like that, as she always came back with different ways we were to do things. I decided I didn't want to be a leader, it involved far too many meetings.

At the end of one of the weeks there, the two girls asked me if I would like to go out with them on Sunday after church. I was so excited, but when I asked Aunty K she said it was not a good idea as I might say things I shouldn't when off guard and relaxed. I was so upset, but later she said that perhaps it would be possible in a few more weeks, when I was more settled into my life as Anna. I could not understand why it mattered so much, especially as we were in a different country to that of my birth.

The next day I thanked the girls but said that Aunty K had plans for me, and that maybe I could go another time. They both smiled, but I thought I saw a strange look come across Natalya's face, just for a second, then decided that it must have been my imagination. Yana was all smiles and said she quite understood as her family were always planning things for her, and not always the things she wanted to do.

Chapter Four

Happy Days

The following weeks were very busy as the firm had taken on a new contract with a country called Italy. I loved hearing about all of the new places and hoped that one day I would be able to travel to some of them myself.

The two girls remained friendly, but I always felt guarded around Natalya. She was very nice, cheerful and friendly, but there was something that made me feel uneasy. I did not mention it to Aunty K, as I knew from experience that anything out of the ordinary would result in me being moved away. I wasn't sure if there were any more aunties in other places, I hoped not. For the first time since I was very young, I felt settled.

Once a year, in the summer, there was a big outdoor party for all of the workers. Because I only saw the people from my office, I thought they were the whole staff, but no, there were lots of other offices, all of whom gathered together for the party.

I was allowed to go but only after a very strict talking to by Aunty K, who also came as parents and guardians were allowed to attend. I was very disappointed not to go alone, but I was determined to get some time by myself. I told the girls that Aunty K would be coming. Yana said that she would introduce her to her mother, Natalya said nothing.

The day came and we put on our best clothes ready for the party. Aunty K looked so different when dressed up, so young and beautiful. Like my mother would have looked, I thought. No wonder that the travelling fair people wanted her to go with them. As we were getting ready I asked her about that time of her life. I didn't really think that she would talk about it, but she did.

The fair had come to the village and Aunty K, who was then 18 years old, was as excited as the other girls to be going. Everyone dressed in their fancy clothes and spent the evening visiting different stalls and rides. Aunty K and her friend Svetlana went to have their palms read by one of the gypsies, in a small red tent near to where the horses were tethered.

On their way to the tent, one of the horses got spooked and reared up, unsettling the horse next to it. The result was total confusion and a dangerous situation. Without a thought, Aunty K went straight to the panicking stallion and calmed him down with her soothing words. He gradually relaxed, as did the rest of the team. By this time, several of the men had appeared and watched in awe as Aunty K talked to the beautiful creature, patting him, and him nuzzling her in return.

A young man of about 20 stepped forward and told her that this was his horse and that he was grateful that she had saved him from injury. With a nod of the head, she and her friend went on with their outing. The next night they went again to the fair, where the young man sought them out. At the end of the week when the fair left, the young man and Aunty K went too. I loved the story, it was so romantic.

This young man was my Uncle Stephan who sadly had died at 28 after an accident putting up one of the rides. Aunty K was too heartbroken to go on without him and so had made her home in Brasov, their last stop together.

After hearing this story, many aspects of Aunty K's demeanour made more sense to me. Although Aunty K mostly seemed happy and carefree, there was a sadness in her eyes that I could occasionally see when she thought no one was looking.

The party was exciting, I had never been to a party before, there was so much noise, food and dancing. The shipping company was enormous, I had never seen that many people together in one place, mostly young and all enjoying themselves. A young man asked me to dance but I said no because I did not know how to dance and was happy to watch the other couples swirling around the flattened ground.

There was a small band playing, with five members – one with a piano accordion, one a violin, one a small drum, one a mandolin and one a guitar. They all sang happy songs with a rhythm so lively that you could not keep your feet still. All wore colourful costumes, it was wonderful.

Aunty K was talking to my supervisor, the one who Natalya had all the meetings with, and out of the corner of my eye I saw my two friends beckoning to me. I didn't think that it would do any harm to wander away for a few minutes, so I went over to them. Natalya spoke first, she wanted me to meet some of her other friends. Yana was there too so I felt that it would be alright. There was another girl and three young men who were standing talking. I was a little apprehensive but also excited to be meeting other people as my world was very small and had been that way since I was a child.

After all of the hellos, we started to talk about ourselves. I had to be very careful that I only told them what Aunty K had taught me to say. One of the boys seemed particularly interested and said that he recognised my accent because his grandparents were originally from that part of the world. I told him that I had moved when I was young to live with Aunty K. He asked what had happened to my parents and I was able to answer him honestly and say that I did not know. I had been orphaned and had lived with my aunts. He seemed to accept that and asked no more questions. This was a party after all, and I wanted to enjoy myself. I told the girls that I was going back to find Aunty K as she would be worrying about me.

I quickly left, and while walking back I began to wonder if it really had been a chance encounter or whether there was something more sinister behind it. I was wary, probably because I had spent my whole childhood and early teens being very secretive. My real name was still unknown to them, for which I was glad.

Back with Aunty K, I began to relax and enjoy the party. I did not tell her about the meeting with the others. Aunty K did not like Natalya and told me to be careful around her. However, she did like Yana, for which I was relieved. After all, I did need some friends.

I found out later why there were so many people there. I had thought that our company was the only one, but that was not true. We were a sub-office and the main one was in Constanța, which of course made much more sense. Constanța was a port on the edge of the Black Sea. All of the actual shipping went from there. There was another office up in the north of the country, at Suceava in Moldova. This, I was to later learn, was a border area, part of the Austrian Empire at one time, and many German-speaking peoples had migrated there. The party was held in a different place each year. This was very exciting, the world suddenly seemed big again.

The young man, called Hans, asked me again to dance and this time I said yes, but told him that I did not know how. He said he would show me and off we went to join the other dancers. I loved it, twirling around the floor, spinning and rocking, it was exhilarating. He held me tightly so that I did not fall, and I felt very safe in his arms. I did not want it to stop. Suddenly I was having experiences that I had missed throughout my life. I was not angry at my aunties, they were doing what they could for me, and also I knew that all of the secrecy was because of my parents. How I longed to know the truth.

Chapter Five

Work and Play

Life went back to normal after the party, with everyone reminiscing about the night and planning for the next one. I felt really settled with Aunty K, and one winter's eve, while relaxing and drinking our hot berry juice by the fire, I decided to ask again about my parents.

She was very reluctant at first but as I was now 17 felt that I was adult enough to know the truth. She said she only knew about the early part of their lives as she had left home when very young. My father was from one of the surrounding villages and the families vaguely knew of each other. He and my mother met at the large produce market and fair that visited the area every year. Aunty K had gone with her sisters, Aunty A and my mother Natasha, known to everyone as Tasha. They had first properly laid eyes on each other as they awaited their turn on the Ferris wheel. It was instant love. His name was Sergei, she was 16 and he was 18.

My mother was still at school, but my father had left to be an apprentice engineer at the local factory. Everyone thought that the factory produced farming machinery and implements, which was mainly true, but it was later found to have a secret research section. No one knew why or what it was for, and if Aunty K did know she was not going to tell me. However, she did say that she thought this was where my father had worked for the four years that he was there. During this time they had married, and I was born.

There had been many workers at the factory, then suddenly one day they were all told to go home, and the factory gates were locked. My parents disappeared the next day, sadly leaving me with Aunty A. That, said Aunty K, was all that she knew.

It did answer some of my questions, but it did not explain why they had never been back to the village, or even heard of for the last almost 20 years. It also did not explain why I had to keep my identity secret or why I was moved on every time I made some friends.

I would lie in my bed at night making up many stories, wondering if any of them could be true. Sometimes my parents were famous scientists who discovered something they shouldn't have, sometimes they were spies on a secret mission, but for who or where, I did not know. Sometimes they were just young lovers who had run away, and sometimes, sadly, I thought that they had died, like my grandparents, no longer around to talk to and answer my many questions. It was certainly a puzzle, and I longed to know the answer. Work days were very busy and the days passed by quickly. I still had my lunches with Natalya and Yana, and I found out that the boy I had danced with had been transferred to our company, but in a different office. I would see him occasionally and he would wave to me. I did not tell Aunty K.

It was early December, soon to be the celebration of Sfântul Nicolae. Traditionally, children would leave out their shoes in the hope that they would receive sweets and small gifts for being good throughout the year. Everyone hoped that they would not wake to find them full of coal and wooden sticks, which was said to be left for the naughty ones. I wondered what I would get if I left mine out, but of course I was much too old for that sort of thing, being a grown up young lady of almost 18.

Aunty K announced we were to spend the next few weeks getting ready for Christmas. We spent our time making the decorations and the food. It was customary for neighbours to invite each other into their homes. It was the time of the year that I enjoyed most. I loved all the colours, decorating the house, the lovely food, and of course the presents.

The time came when we were to have some days away from our work to celebrate the festivities with our families. Hans came to find me during our lunch break to wish me happiness over the Christmas and New Year, and said he would see me next year. He said the same to Natalya and Yana, but I knew it was really for me. I had grown to like him very much, and though we rarely spoke I knew he liked me. I had had male friends before, Tomas and Petyr, but this felt different. I wanted to tell Aunty K, but could not bear to think that I would be moved on again. I felt fully settled and liked living in this happy home.

We concentrated on making our Christmas celebrations the best ever. One evening we went to the Christmas market in the town square. It was magical, hundreds of lanterns casting their light on the stalls and the people, making strange shadows in the night.

There was music, and a man dressed as a goat, as was tradition, playing the fool and making everyone laugh. Some stalls sold food and the smells were just so inviting. We bought some gogosi, a treat resembling little donuts, and ate them as we wandered about the square. I hoped that I would see Hans, but was relieved, deep down, when we didn't. It would require too much explaining to Aunty K. I was now used to the idea that I had to keep some of my friends secret.

We started to feel very cold so decided to go home, our magical night coming to an end. Well, not quite to an end, as we had a warming cup of hot chocolate before bed.

I looked to see Hans at work but he had already left for his home in the far north of the country. His home, as I had lately found out, was in Suceava, part of Moldova. The other shipping office was located there, and I realised that he must have been on loan and so the chances of seeing him again were very small.

I was so excited. Up until now my Christmases had been quite solitary affairs, as neither Aunty A nor Aunty E had made much of the celebrations. Aunty K was so different, she was light, airy and fun. I loved her dearly.

Chapter Six

Christmas and Questions

Christmas Eve came and we finished decorating the house. The town's children had come, carrying their stars on poles. This was a lovely tradition where each star was made from tinsel and coloured paper, and carried from house to house. The beautiful Star Carol was sung at each door.

"The star has appeared on high,
Like a big secret in the sky,
The star is so bright,
May all of your wishes turn out right"

Christmas Day was peaceful, filled with good food and laughter. Aunty K made me my favourite soup, ciorba de pui, full of plump chicken pieces. We talked about what Christmas meant to us, about our present life, and what the future may hold.

With the celebrations done, it was back to work, with much excited talk of who did what, where and with whom over the break. There was also much talk about presents. Aunty K had given me a locket, which I wore with pride. She said it was a family tradition to pass it down when a young woman reached 18, and was to carry a picture of my true love, whenever it was that

I met him. That seemed a long way off as I never really got to know anyone for very long.

I thought of my first friend, Tomas, the hard-working fisherman from my village near the lake. I missed him and our talks by the lakeside. I also thought of the other boys I had met, Petyr, the boys in the Moscow tunnels, and even Hans. Though I had only known them for a short time, I felt my life was richer for having met them.

Natalya and Yana had enjoyed their holiday, and told me of the big family gatherings that had taken place. I felt a little envious, and yet I knew that Aunty K and I had had a lovely time. She still really missed Stephan and their travelling life with the fair. I wondered if she would ever marry again, but at the moment she seemed content to be here with me.

One spring day, Hans reappeared. He had been sent to our office to open a new section. I wondered if he would remember me, but when he saw me he was just as friendly as he had been at the party. Natalya, Yana and I had been chosen to work with him. The new department was to ship goods to England and then out to a place called America. It was all very exciting. I had not realised that the world was so big, and where was this place, America? We had to learn a new language, English, so we could understand the shipping instructions.

Part of each working day was spent learning new words. We had new equipment too, a telegraph machine and a telephone whereby you could speak to people a long way away. We were all a little afraid of the contraption and at first only Hans was allowed to use it. Mostly it was just messages from Constanţa, but occasionally it was from somewhere else, which caused great excitement in the office.

I told Aunty K about it, and though interested, she told me to be very careful what I said into it because you did not know who was listening. Aunty K also had her own work. She looked after the horses belonging to a family living in a large house on the edge of town. I thought that they must be very rich.

One day I fell ill and did not go to work, so after Aunty K had left I started to again look for any clues about my parents. I felt bad about going through her things but my need for answers was so much stronger.

I found the paintings again, including one of three girls in front of a small wooden house, which had faded with age. Were these my aunts?

On the back of one of them were some markings that I hadn't taken notice of the last time. There were no words, just a mix of numbers and letters – 40 .71 :74 .06., G.B (2) 1854. I thought it very strange. I wrote them down in my diary then carefully put everything back in place. Aunty K was very good to me and I knew that this would destroy her trust in me. Later I puzzled and puzzled over the numbers, but could make no sense of them. The next day I felt much better and went back to work. The two girls were very friendly and concerned that I had been ill.

They told me that some official-looking men had been to the office. They had spoken with our supervisor for some time, then came around looking at all of the desks. It did not sound good to me, so I was glad that I had been at home. I was worried that they might come back again, but they did not during the rest of my time there. The office was strangely quiet that day but gradually as time went by people began to relax again.

I was not sure whether to mention it to Aunty K, so for the first few days I said nothing. I really did not want to be moved on again. She must have heard about it from someone else because after a week she asked me what was going on. Reluctantly, I told her about the visit of the two men, but said I thought they were from the head office in Constanța.

As I had been at home that day, there was not very much I could tell her. She seemed satisfied, but told me that now more than ever I must be on my guard and be very careful about what I said to anyone. *Please, please,*

I screamed in my head, *please tell me why*, but outwardly I just nodded and said I would be very careful. I was hoping that Aunty K and I would have another relaxed night so that I could ask her more questions, but that looked unlikely, especially after the official visit.

One morning I was told to go to the supervisor's office. I was so worried, what had I done? Nothing that I could think of. I was so nervous. She was there with a small man who glared over his glasses. He spoke very softly; I could hardly hear him. His accent was strange and even though he spoke Romanian it sounded vaguely Russian, though not from my part of Russia. I could hear Aunty K's voice in my head telling me to take great care.

He began, he wanted to know about Hans. My friend Hans, who I had not seen for a couple of weeks now. I told him that we had not spoken for about two weeks and that I only saw him at work. This was not strictly true as sometimes we met up on the road home. We occasionally spoke of our childhoods, although I had never told him my real name. I so wanted to, but I realised that I could not, although why and who I was protecting I still did not know.

The man said very little, just nodding his head from time to time. I decided that I did not like him very much, he made me feel extremely uncomfortable. After what seemed like a very long time, Mrs Leminski, the supervisor, said I could go back to my desk. I was shaking as I walked down the corridor. I would definitely have to tell Aunty K about this.

I asked my two friends if the man had spoken with them. They both said no but I felt that Natalya was not telling the truth. Yana said very little. I hated all of this secrecy and longed for a normal life, whatever that was.

Chapter Seven

Confessions

The day felt very long, but eventually it was time to go home. Aunty K was not there when I arrived, so I busied myself getting our evening meal ready. I decided that it was time that I was completely honest with her, a decision that would have a dramatic impact on my relationship with her, and on the rest of my life.

Aunty K said very little as I poured out all of my feelings about my life, my parents, moving from place to place, and about Hans. I cried as I told her about seeing the paintings and I cried because I knew I had broken her trust. I felt truly wretched. After I had spoken and a long time had passed in silence, she said, not unkindly, that she would need to think about all of these revelations and then decide what to do.

I went to my room and sat on the bed, weeping so much that I thought that I would wash away. After an hour she called me in to see her. I had already started to pack my things as I was certain that she would send me away.

The house was so quiet and all I could hear was the loud ticking of the old clock on the mantel. She too had been crying, I could see from the water droplets on her face. She started to speak, and my stomach began to hurt. I could feel my breathing speed up. I was so afraid of what might happen now. When she spoke her voice was soft, not angry as I had imagined, but I could hear the disappointment in it.

She said she could understand my need to find out about my parents, as she too had been left alone, although in her case it was a husband who had died. She said that she realised it must have been hard for me, never really having anywhere to settle, not being able to make friends, and the few that I did, I inevitably had to leave behind. She also said that she was angry with me for going through her things and that trust had now been damaged between us. It was dreadful, and I was so sorry, but equally I was desperate to know what had happened, and what was still happening.

We made some tea and sat cradling the ornate cups, the ones from the dresser that we only used for special occasions. As I felt the soothing liquid warm me, she spoke again. Throughout all of this time I just sat and silently wept. I could not bear it if she was to send me away again, my whole life had been a series of uncertainties and moves. I had enjoyed some of the time spent with Aunty A and Aunty E, but I never truly felt happy until I was with Aunty K.

Eventually she said it was time to face up to some truths. She told me that everything that had been done was done to protect me, but it had never really been taken into consideration that I would become more curious as I grew older. Once I reached 21, I could apply for my own papers and go off searching for myself. I had never thought of that, and even though the idea was appealing I did not want to search alone.

She said that she had told me everything that she knew, but would be willing for us both to go through her things together to see if we could find any more clues. I was so relieved, I went to her and threw my arms around her and sobbed loudly. I loved my Aunty K, and no more so than in that moment.

After a very fretful night, I awoke with puffy eyes. At breakfast, Aunty K told me to get ready for my work, bathe my eyes and say nothing to anyone, especially Natalya and Yana. Aunty K was friendly with a relative of Yana's and had been told that that Yana was talking a lot about me and asking lots of questions. At first I thought she meant Natalya, but no, she meant Yana. I was shocked, I had always felt that it was Yana who was on my side. Aunty K said that I was going to have to be a good actress and carry on as normal so as not to arouse any suspicion.

I asked if she knew anything about Hans, and she said that as far as she knew he was of no danger to me. I was glad, I needed at least one friend that I could trust, but of course that did not go so far as telling him my real name and background.

Work went very slowly, and I found it hard to concentrate. I told everyone that I was tired, having slept badly. The girls and I had lunch together and fortunately the conversation was the normal chatter. I was glad that this was the end of the working week so that I would have time at home with Aunty K, and also that I would not have to be on my guard with the two girls.

Aunty K had by then stopped coming to meet me, so I walked slowly home alone, except for the jumble of thoughts that filled my head. Now that Aunty K had had some time to think about everything, would she still tell me to leave, and if so, where would I go? Surely I had run out of aunties by now.

We ate our meal in silence, each, I suppose, waiting for the other to speak. I started by telling her about my day and how I had found it difficult with the two girls now that I knew I had to be even more careful with what I said. I was so disappointed, I thought I had made some real friends. Aunty K suddenly announced that I would be moving on, and after the look of shock on my face, added that she would be coming with me. The time had come to find some answers.

She had been secretly making arrangements. The story we were to use was that she was going to look for Stephan's family, and that it would take some time with them being fair folk. Come Monday, she would go to my work and tell them that I was leaving in two weeks.

I said nothing, as this was a scene that had been played out at various times in my life. At least this time I would not be alone.

Chapter Eight

On the Road

The following two weeks were a flurry of packing what was needed for the trip and sorting out the house, which was to be left in the care of a friend, Maria. *So she does intend to come back here*, I thought, and I wondered if that included me.

My last day at work was a mixture of sadness and excitement. Everyone wanted to know where we were going, I answered them honestly and said that I did not know. Natalya and Yana hugged me and said that they hoped to see me again someday. I looked for Hans, but he was not there, so once again I was unable to say goodbye to a friend. That saddened me more than anything.

The next day, very early, a horse and cart came for us. We loaded on our belongings and with a last goodbye to Maria, and the town, we left. I felt really bad as I knew this was because of me, but I did not understand why. Sometimes ignorance could be a soft velvety blanket to wrap yourself in, but other times it could be a thorn that pricked you every time you relaxed. I did not ask where we were going, sadly my closeness to Aunty K was not fully repaired, though she was not unfriendly. Silent tears rolled down my face as we left the small town behind.

We arrived at the train station minutes before the train arrived to carry us northwards. Even though it was still early morning, there were many people on the train. I supposed that they were going to their work, there can't have been many like us who were running away.

To my surprise we only went about two stops. We quickly jumped off and watched the train as it continued on its way. A few others had alighted and like them we crossed the tracks and started to walk towards the village just visible in the distance. I was intrigued, I had thought that we were going on a long journey to another country, but no, it was just two villages away.

Aunty K seemed happier this morning and hummed to herself as we walked along the narrow country roads. We passed a man coming the other way who seemed to know Aunty K. He raised his hat and wished us a good morning. Even though there was no lake here, it made me nostalgic. I asked Aunty K where we were going, but she just smiled and said I would know when we got there. My trunk began to feel really heavy and I wished I had not brought so much luggage, it wasn't as if I had not travelled before, I had had plenty of practice.

After an hour of walking we could see the church spire and roofs of the small houses of the village. There were a few farms dotted across the landscape, the workers already busy sowing the seeds, making ready for the autumn harvest. Cows stood silently in the fields, patiently waiting for milking. I was glad that I was not a farmer, their work was very hard and the days very long. I would have liked to work at the lakeside with my friends like Tomas, who I thought of most days. He must be a man now, I thought, and I wondered if he had married and had a family. At 15, I thought that he would marry me, but here I was at 18, unmarried and moving on again. I had enjoyed my adventures, but I longed for some stability and a place to call home.

We arrived at a timber house on the edge of the village and Aunty K knocked on the door. An elderly lady answered, and on seeing Aunty K threw her arms around her. There was joy and tears and I stood and watched in amazement. Aunty K knew so many people. This was Margarite, the mother of the two men that we had come to see. She told us where her sons Atila and Bebe were working. They were horse handlers and had also worked with the fair people. Like their mother, they were very pleased to see us. I think they thought that I was Aunty K's daughter, so we did not tell them differently.

The men were working at the smithy on the other side of the village, shoeing a very large horse. I had never seen such a creature, he was magnificent. Taller than me, his coat gleaming black except for the white socks around his hooves. He stood patiently as they lifted each leg to attach a new shoe. They told me not to be afraid as he was a very gentle beast despite his size.

When they had finished they beckoned me over to say hello to him. I went to him slowly with the apple they had given me for him. He took it from me then nuzzled his head into my shoulder. We were firm friends from that moment on. While this was going on, Aunty K had gone to speak with the older of the two brothers, Atila. After what seemed a very long while, she came back and said we were to go back into the village and wait at the mother's house.

Chapter Nine

Our New Home

On our return there was freshly baked bread and thick vegetable soup awaiting us. Before too long the brothers appeared, and we sat and enjoyed the delicious food set out in front of us.

They were such warm, welcoming people. I felt at ease with them. Later we went to the back of the house to find the large black horse hitched to a cart. The cart had a green canopy with a yellow gold trim. From the outside the cart looked really small, but once inside it seemed much bigger.

This, Aunty K informed me, was to be our home once we were out on the road. I felt a mixture of dismay and excitement, this was not how I had envisioned my life when we left the town, but the pull of the road, going off into the unknown on an adventure that could take us anywhere, was truly invigorating.

With our preparations under way, we went to the village market to buy the provisions needed, for us and for the horse, who I named Hercules. There were so many things to think about as the journey was to take several weeks. Where we were going was still a mystery, but Aunty K was certainly used to this way of life.

The cart was to be filled with everything needed – bed boards, bedding, pots and other provisions. It looked so crowded that I wondered if there would be room for us. Aunty K laughed and told me that the cooking would be done outside and on fine warm nights we would sleep outside. I wasn't quite sure how I felt about that.

I watched in awe as the little caravan, as we called it, was made ready to travel. Everything was packed neatly into its own space and there emerged a fully functional "home", finished off with a heavy, highly decorative curtain at the doorway, to pull across at night. Maybe my parents had run away in such a way, I thought, and here I was, following in their footsteps.

All we needed to do now was plan our route. Aunty K, Margarite and the two men sat down to talk about the best way to cover the distance to our next stop. I also sat in on this, but said nothing, I only listened. They had all travelled this route, and many others, when they had been with the fair. After a while, I excused myself and went out to see Hercules who was quietly grazing outside of the house.

I sat on a grassy mound, comforted by the gentle presence of the large horse who was to become a major part of my life. I thought about everything that had brought me to this point. The happy days down by the lake, watching the activities of the fishermen, spending time with Tomas. So much laughter and talk of the future.

I thought about my time with stern Aunty Elena in her underground home. I thought about my enjoyment of our few trips to market, relieved to be out in the sunshine, then my fear and upset at being told I had to move on again, this time to yet another aunty, and worse still, in another country. And lastly I thought about Aunty K, whom I had come to love with all of my heart. My fears had come to nothing, and I had been living with the most amazing person that I had ever met. She cared for me, sharing my bad days when my worries overtook me and my good days when life felt much more joyful. And now she had given up everything to help me in my quest.

I sat, deep in thought, for what seemed an eternity. Eventually, Aunty K reappeared, plans in place. It was time to say goodbye to our friendly, helpful hosts. Finally we were ready to set off.

Part Two
"The Journey"

Chapter Ten

Sighişoara

Our first stop was to be Sighişoara. This had nothing to do with my parents, it was a nostalgia trip for Aunty K. She and Stephan had stayed there when she first came to Romania. She spoke of it so fondly, with a faraway look in her eyes. I could see that she had some good memories of the place and I certainly was not going to spoil things.

This was a small town about 30km away from the village. We were to take things very slowly to allow the horse, Hercules, to get to know us, and us him.

Aunty K was wonderful with horses, but I was surprised that he liked me too. Perhaps it was the apple that I gave him that made him more trustful of me. Often it was me who led him while Aunty K busied herself. Doing what, I wasn't quite sure.

The narrow roads were very quiet, sometimes hardly more than tracks. The first signs of spring were starting to show as the fields had shed their winter coats. I could easily understand why people liked this style of life. An old train rattled past us in the distance and we saw occasional villages with their small collection of houses, and in the middle the church with its spires standing tall.

The first evening we stopped, Aunty K showed me how to attend to Hercules, how to detach him from the cart, how to groom and feed him, before settling him for the night, usually tethered to a nearby tree. I was a little afraid of him, he was such a large horse, but his gentle breathing and nuzzling soon told me that I had nothing to fear. He became my friend and guardian and I knew that we would be safe with him. Aunty K told me that I had a way with horses and that it must be a family trait as this was her particular gift.

The large cooking pot was soon over the fire and we made some delicious soup from the vegetables and dried meat we had brought. Later we sat out under the stars and talked. It was the best talk we had had since all of the upset. I was relieved as I loved her very much and was sorry to have broken her trust. It was a fine night, so, snuggled in our blankets, we settled down in the little wooded area that was our first stopover. I felt safe with Hercules nearby, knowing that he would alert us to any danger.

The night passed peacefully and in the morning we made ready to move northwards. Not long after dawn we were on our way. We exchanged hellos with everyone we met on the road, waved at the workers in the fields, and stopped in some of the villages to buy bread and vegetables. If this was life on the road, then I liked it. Of course, there were days when the weather turned against us, so we sheltered where we could and slept inside.

Before too long we reached our destination, the mediaeval town where Aunty K and Stephan had spent many happy days. We started to meet up with people who knew Aunty K and who were surprised to see her. We went to a wooded area just outside of the town border where we were to spend the next few nights. There were already some other caravans there making a merry little encampment.

Wonderful smells of food cooking in the large pots greeted us. Hercules settled and we made our own soup, borsch, a warm and wholesome reminder of our homeland. Having eaten, and night having fallen, the camp suddenly came alive with music and dancing, the men playing their fiddles, the women dancing, their skirts swirling in time to the music, all set against the flickering fires near each caravan. Shadows danced against the night sky, it was magical. I just sat and watched, my eyes wide with the wonderment of it all. Aunty K did not dance that first night but sat with glistening eyes, remembering her life from the past.

Some of the people left at first light but many, like us, stayed for at least one more night. We were to go to the town for supplies and to visit some old friends of Aunty K. All of the horses were left tethered, in the care of those chosen to stay at the camp.

I was interested to see the town and I was not disappointed. We went through the town gate with a dark tower above it. Strange small painted figures rotated around the clock face. I felt a little apprehensive as I knew from my history lessons that this was where a mighty prince had lived, a blood thirsty warrior, still said to defend his territory. Aunty K sensed my fear, put her arm around me and laughed gaily as we walked to the main square.

The town was so old, with cobbled streets, tiled roofs and many small shops selling all that we needed. We passed down a narrow alley with small houses painted in many colours on our way to the candle makers. Aunty K had brought some of her beautiful things from home to trade for the goods that we needed.

Near the square there was a covered stairway leading up to the church. A strange lady dressed all in white sat on one of the steps, strumming her strange instrument and singing even stranger music. It unnerved me, but I think that Aunty K had seen her before. We met a young woman with flowing black hair, large blue eyes and an ample bosom, who obviously knew Aunty K and rushed up and flung her arms around her. She, Valentina, had also travelled with the fair. We went to her rooms, and over many cups of tea, and I suspect a little alcohol, the two women became girls again as they talked of the past.

Chapter Eleven

Revelations

We made ready for our next move, joined in with the night's festivities and fell asleep under the stars.

At first light we left and continued northwards. I marvelled at how Aunty K knew the way, but she said you just follow the sun and the stars. We wandered along narrow lanes with me leading Hercules, who trotted patiently beside me. I really loved the big horse, his hooves singing on the tracks, his fine mane swaying with his movement, his magnificent tail swishing away any insects, and his gentle breathing as he moved beside me.

We walked on, passing fields that stretched out for as far as I could see. Already the farm labourers were out tending to the livestock and preparing the crops ready for the harvest later in the year. We travelled past various villages, catching glimpses of the red-tiled church roofs and the many farms dotted across the countryside.

Each night we found a safe place to stop, and after food we bedded down. Aunty K had a lightness about her, and I could see that here on the road was where she had been most happy. Sometimes we talked and other times were spent in comfortable silence.

Her stories were mostly of being on the road and travelling with the fair, of Stephan and the other fair folk. She missed her husband very much and it was easy to see how in love they had been. Occasionally she spoke of my mother and of the three sisters growing up in the village by the lake. It sounded like an idyllic life to me, I had known nothing but change and moving on.

My mother was the middle sister, and the prettiest (according to Aunty K), and it was she who had married first, to the clever young man at the factory. He was liked by all of the girls, but it was my mother who had won his heart. A wedding had taken place, with my mother making the most beautiful bride. Only Aunty Elena had come from my father's family, but he was happy that his sister had come. When the wedding ceremony was over, the celebrations went on into the night. I was born less than a year after, and it was three years later that they disappeared, leaving me with

Aninya, Aunty A, my mother's eldest sister. Aunty K was too young at the time to look after me.

One thing I had always wondered about was my strange name, my real name. Aunty K said that perhaps it was some sort of code, but exactly what, no one knew, or at least no one had worked out yet. I had always thought that too, and was certain that at some point all would become clear to me. It just seemed to be taking such a long time. Aunty K said that we would be making our way back to Russia where, hopefully, we would find some answers. I asked her about the bracelet that Aunty A had given me, the one with the little animals on it. Sadly, Aunty K knew nothing about it, so that was another mystery that would have to wait to be solved.

The journey was a happy one and I loved seeing the countryside, even on the days when it rained. On these times we would snuggle up in the caravan, after making sure that Hercules was sheltered under the trees. I felt that I could live like this forever, but of course it would come to an end all too soon.

After several days travelling, past places with exotic names, we started to see the churches and houses of a larger town, which Aunty K informed me was Suceava. I had heard of it as it was the place where Hans lived, he had talked much about it. Would I see him? I did hope so. I reminded Aunty K of my friendship with Hans and that the shipping company had an office here, but as always she already knew, just as she seemed to know about everything else.

This town was actually a city, the only other one I had seen was Moscova. It had many large buildings, including the big grey and white one where the shipping office was located. We also saw a fortress and a very old clock tower. We walked on to where we would stay for the night. Again there were many other caravans encamped, so I knew that we would be in for a happy, noisy night.

Aunty K said she would go back into the centre to see what information she could find out. I was to stay with Hercules and the caravan. I was disappointed not to go too, but during the time spent on the road Hercules had become my responsibility and I had come to love him. I begged Aunty K to let me know any news of my friend.

She was gone for a long time and I had begun to worry for her safety. Finally she reappeared and with her was a person I knew well. Hans. I was so pleased to see him. Aunty K left us to talk while she prepared our meal. He told me that after he had spoken with the sinister small man with the glasses, he was told to go back north to his own office and stay there until contacted again. The man, he felt, was a policeman so he had been very guarded in what he said. I remembered the man well, he had made me feel very uncomfortable and a little afraid.

During the meal, Hans began to speak more freely. He was not just a random person sent down to the Brasov office, he had volunteered because he knew I was there. He was part of a network of people who knew Aunty K and my parents. I realised it was not by coincidence that I had gone to work at the shipping office. It became clear that Natalya was indeed my friend and that she had adopted the antagonistic role to keep Yana away from learning the truth.

It was all too much, I really did not know who to trust. I knew it was to protect me and yet I felt more alone than ever. I listened quietly as Hans talked, disappointed because I had really liked him and thought that he liked me for me.

The network had been set up many years before when Aunty K and Stephan had travelled through the countryside with the fair. The family of Hans had also been with the fair and had settled in Suceava with some of their German relatives. Hans had been sworn to secrecy when he found out that his parents were part of the circle dedicated to keeping the secrets and looking after my parents and me.

Chapter Twelve

Road to Odesa

After the meal, Hans asked to speak to me alone. We walked some way from the camp, not too far, but far enough not to be overheard. He said that he wanted me to know that he really cared about me and that he had not expected to when he came down to our office. His feelings, he said, were genuine and he hoped that he and I could remain friends and perhaps something more in the future.

I was too stunned to speak. Even though everything had been done for my sake, I felt betrayed by them all. And still I had no real answers. We walked back slowly to the caravan and I asked to be excused. I could hear his voice in very low tones talking to Aunty K, but as to what they were saying, I could not really hear. I stayed in the caravan for the rest of the evening, only coming out to bed down Hercules, my one true friend.

Aunty K busied herself around the camp, smiling over at me occasionally, but thankfully she left me to my own thoughts. In the darkness I went again to see Hercules. He laid his big head on my shoulder and gently nuzzled me. I felt a calmness come over me and I knew that I was now ready to face anything. Surely there could be no more shattering revelations.

Aunty K called me and said that we needed to discuss what was to happen next. I couldn't stay angry with her as she had done everything to help me with what was now my quest. She asked me to forgive Hans as he did care for me and all of his actions had been to help and protect me.

We spoke for some time and I asked her how it was that so many people were involved. She said that my parents had come to the fair one day, many years after they had disappeared, saying how heartbroken they were about everything, especially having to leave me behind. Aunty K and Stephan said that they would help to keep the secret and to set up a network of people to help me, should the occasion ever arise. They were all fair people who had settled in different areas. I asked how they all managed to keep in touch with each other, but the explanation was simple. The fair still travelled around every year and visited all of the places where people had made their homes. No matter where they were, these people were still part of the community. Aunty K and I were following the route taken by the fair. Of course, this was why the fair only visited once a year, there were such great distances to cover. I knew that Aunty K knew many people, I had not realised just how many.

Aunty K was famous throughout the fair world because of her skills with horses, and also because of Stephan who was well loved and deeply mourned. The fire burned low as we got ready for sleep. Tomorrow was going to be a momentous day.

We were on our way back to Russia and needed to reach Odesa, a port on the Black Sea. It was from here that we would board a train to take us to Moscova. Hans was to travel with us, and later he would take ownership of Hercules and return with him and the caravan to Suceava, to await the return of Aunty K.

We still had many days travel through Moldova, but our route was made easier by the help we received from Hans and the different villages along the way. There was a strange feeling of foreboding in the air, although no one knew why. Life in the villages went on the same, but there was an uneasiness in the towns and the cities.

Aunty K said it reminded her of a time many years ago when fighting had broken out and there were strikes throughout the country. The Tsar had made concessions, and a new government was formed. We later heard a rumour that, somewhere in the south, a personage of great rank had been assassinated.

I was worried, and even though Aunty K said that it shouldn't affect us as we were travelling north, I could see that she was worried. We finally reached Odesa without incident, and it was time to say goodbye to Hans and Hercules. I did not know who I was going to be most sorry to see go, the big gentle horse or Hans, who I had come to be more at ease with over the past few weeks. I realised that he had given up much to come with us, including his job and his home. I was grateful.

The day had come, and after a very emotional farewell, we boarded the train. I hoped that I would see them again, but that would be down to fate, good luck and circumstance. We did not have much luggage as Aunty

K had sold many of her things to finance the trip, and I had got rid of my trunk. What was left went with Hans and Hercules.

The train journey was to take several days, so we settled into our seats in the carriage that we were sharing with a family who were moving back to Moscova. I cannot say that we got much sleep, as the family were very lively, especially the two young boys. They must have been around 10 and 11, and wanted to know about everything, especially us. We kept to our story that our names were Katya and Anna and we too were moving back to Moscova. I did not feel that they posed any threat to us, and so felt relaxed during the trip. The parents spent their time seeing to the boys. Aunty K was cautious, but then she always was. Even though I had moved around a lot, I was still naïve in the ways of the world, so the best thing was for me to stay quiet. Not unfriendly, just quiet.

The scenery was much like Romania, with forests, villages and the odd town. We all shared our food and in the evenings talked until tiredness overcame us. It was a pleasant trip, but with some sadness as I knew it was taking me further and further away from Hans. It was very confusing, as I knew I wanted to find out about my parents, but also I realised how much I cared about Hans. We stopped at a town called Vinnytsia. We did not get off the train as we had enough supplies for the whole journey, and also it was safer to stay out of sight.

Aunty K began to talk about the lake and how life had been so simple until the young fishermen started to disappear. Many years later, she was to learn that they had been abducted to join the army. She said that the same feeling was in the air now, although no one knew why. Tomas and I had just thought it was a myth, one of the mysteries of the lake. We used to sing songs about it, including *Glorious Sea* that everyone knew. We knew very little of the world and the cruelty of one man against another.

Aunty Elena, who we were on our way to see, knew most about these events. Living in the capital city, she was able to find out much more information.

Chapter Thirteen

Back to Russian Soil

The days went quite slowly, and I learned to sleep even with the noise from the two young boys, Nicki and Alex. The rest of the time was spent staring out of the window, talking and eating. Our supplies lasted us well, sharing with the family, as was the custom on long-distance trains.

We could hear singing further down the train, folk songs like the ones the fishermen used to sing while mending their nets. It filled me with longing for the lake and my past life. If Aunty K felt nostalgic, she did not say. The songs were in a mixture of languages, but the tunes were very familiar.

On one of the days, the boys and I walked through the train to see who else was travelling the route with us. To my surprise, the train was very full, each compartment taken up with many noisy families. A real exodus. There was no one I knew, of which I was pleased. I didn't want to be on my guard all of the time.

At the end of each carriage was a samovar, constantly stoked by the guard, ensuring that there was always hot water for the food and drinks. It reminded me of the train I travelled on when I first left Aunty A to go to the city to be with Aunty E.

The train moved steadily northwards and did not stop much, just at Vinnytsia, and later at a larger city, which Aunty K informed me was the capital of this country. We were told to stay on the train as we pulled into the station. On the other line was a long train, grey and with few windows. Here and there we caught glimpses of soldiers, and on the open wagons were large shapes, covered over, like huge beasts getting ready to pounce.

The atmosphere of the place was awful, the air heavy. With what, I did not know. Eventually we were on our way. No one spoke of what we had seen, it was as if it had not happened.

Slowly we gathered speed and as we got further away from the station, train life went back to normal. The oppressive atmosphere lifted and some of the laughter and song returned. Since we had boarded the train, Aunty K and I had been speaking in Russian, rusty at first, but we soon became at ease with it. It must have been at least three years since we had conversed in our mother tongue.

Some days later we came to a border post and Aunty K and the parents went to present our papers. The children and I stayed in the compartment. They were gone a very long time. On their return they talked about how different it had been this time, crossing the border. There were many more checks, and as Aunty K said, the feeling of foreboding had returned. Some of the young men were being taken off the train. Fortunately the two boys were too young.

We said nothing of the military train we had seen and felt relieved when we finally moved off again, this time on to Russian soil. The rest of the journey passed without incident, with us again spending our time staring out of the windows at the scenery, the trees and the large expanses of farmland. Everywhere the land was being tended for the next harvest, livestock were out on the hills and people were going about their daily toil, dawn until dark.

The scenery began to change as we came to the outskirts of each little town. Compared with the cleanliness and order of the countryside, these areas looked dirty and squalid. I began to wish that we had stayed in Brasov, but of course I did not say anything to Aunty K, as all of this journey was for my sake.

Finally we arrived at the main station in Moscova. We said our goodbyes to our travelling companions, gathered our belongings and stepped off the train. The noise levels were tremendous, with great throngs of people everywhere. As we walked we could hear many different dialects and saw people wearing all manner of dress. I was fascinated, but it also made me very nervous.

Aunty E was not there to meet us, but the arrangement was to meet up at the central market building. I vaguely wondered how she would know to go there, but realised things must have been put into place weeks ago via Aunty K's folk network. It never ceased to amaze me how the whole operation worked. No wonder my parents were able to disappear so completely.

Moscova seemed very different to me, although I had not actually seen very much of it, living hidden away with Aunty E. We travelled on one of the new trams, that had replaced the horse drawn cabbies that I remembered. The market was only a few stops and not too crowded. We found the cafe area and waited for Aunty E to find us.

She had a lightness in her step and when she saw us a large smile spread across her face. Could this be the same Aunty E that I lived with all those years ago? She sat with us and we drank tea. We were to buy food items from the market then go to her new home.

The market was colourful, busy and loud. We wandered around the stalls selling every type of goods that you could imagine – vegetables of every kind, meat stalls, places to buy textiles, pots, pans and items for the home. The austerity in the countryside was not yet evident in the cities, and yet, for all of that, there was a strange feeling in the air.

Aunty E no longer lived underground but had moved into a flat where, I was surprised to hear, she lived with a husband. Once home, she told us of her fortunes since I had left. She had met her husband on one of her trips out at the museum. He, Mikhail, was a professor at the Lomonosov University. There had been a strike there and, following many protests, a large number of the staff and students had left. Her husband had been junior staff at the time and so stayed in his job. He had subsequently been promoted to professor.

They owned a dacha, which was common for people of the middle classes, and this was where we were to stay during our time in the city, which we now were to call Moscow. Aunty K said we were to be careful about talking of our past. Aunty E told us that her husband, though part of the establishment, was in his heart as revolutionary as she. Our story was that we were friends from home, me being Aunty K's daughter, on our way to St Petersburg to visit family.

More secrets. I found it all very difficult and longed for a time when we could be honest about everything.

Chapter Fourteen

Life in the Dacha

We were to stay in the dacha, their summer home in the forest, just outside Moscow. We went straight away. Aunty E said she would take us then return later in the evening with her husband. Once away from the city, we could relax more.

The feeling in the city was uneasy and heavy. We needed to know what was happening. Aunty E began to tell us. The assassination that we had heard about was in Serbia, a relative of the German Kaiser, who had subsequently been persuaded to take retribution for the act. This had upset the allies of Serbia, which included Russia. Any act of aggression from Germany was to be met with resistance from Serbia's friends. This, we realised, was the reason for the soldiers we had seen, and we had heard that the factories had changed to the making of what we now knew to be armaments.

Aunty K said that it should not really affect our plans as we were going further northwards, but it may slow our progress down. We had to be sure to speak Russian at all times.

The dacha was small but suited all of our needs. Having lived in a caravan for several weeks, it felt to me very spacious. Once we had been shown where everything was and introduced to our nearest neighbour, Aunty E went back to Moscow, she was to return in the next few days with Mikhail. The garden was in a sorry state so we set about tidying it and sorting what we could use for food. Aunty K was so clever and seemed to know about everything, and was happy to pass on her knowledge. I learned a lot from her.

As evening fell the fires were lit, and food smells emanated from the different cottages. We had another of our talks before bed, but this one was of a more serious nature. The possible outbreak of a full-scale war put everything into a different light. We would have to be very careful as we travelled onwards, and our mode of dress changed to that of working peasants. We knew we would be required to work the land, ensuring food supplies for the army. This would become increasingly important as the months went by.

Aunty E and the new Uncle M arrived the next evening. He was tall and a few years younger than Aunty E, who was I supposed in her early forties. We were all a little anxious as we did not really know where his sympathies lay. The evening passed off without incident and I was sent to bed while the others talked. I could hear their low tones as I drifted off to sleep.

It seemed that we had nothing to worry about, as Uncle M was actually part of a network that was still in touch with some of the professors and students who had taken part in the strike three years earlier. Secretly, of course, as it would have seriously affected his position at the university and may have resulted in him being arrested and sent to a labour camp in Siberia.

We were to stay in the dacha for the whole of the summer, working the land to feed ourselves and to sell off the excess. The last that Aunty E had heard of her brother and my mother was eight years earlier when they had travelled through Moscow on their way to St Petersburg. I was upset that she had not told me that when I stayed with her, but she must have thought me too young to be trusted with such information.

Mikhail and Aunty E did not come back until their working week had ended, by which time Aunty K and I had settled into country life. It never ceased to amaze me what she knew and what she could do. There were some horses on the site and they soon became part of our lives, grooming them and generally looking after them. Even I helped as I was becoming much more confident with them, in part due to Aunty K, but mostly, I think, thanks to Hercules who taught me that horses, when properly treated, were nothing to be afraid of. I missed him very much.

I liked living in the dacha and went happily about my chores. The other people there, though interested in us at first, soon came to regard us as part of the community. The dachas were mainly allotted to the middle and upper classes, the elite of Moscow society, with most people only being there at the end of the working week.

In September of that year it was announced that Russia would enter the war. Mikhail had been called upon to act as a logistics advisor. The role of women was as yet undefined, but many would later become nurses. We were now faced with the decision as to whether to move on now or wait until the following spring. We would move on in two weeks.

We started our preparations. Many in-depth talks took place with Uncle M and Aunty E. We were to follow the trail to St Petersburg, a port on the gulf of Finland, and which, I was told, was the winter home of the Tsar and his family. This part of the trip would be dangerous as there had been a lot of troop movements and civil unrest.

Mikhail had been able to obtain new papers for us and an address outside of the city to stay in once we arrived. Aunty K and I were to be mother and daughter, returning home to help on the family farm. This would not be difficult to enact as it was much the same as we had been doing since we left Brasov. Oh, those days seemed so long ago.

During one of our evening talks, my real name had been mentioned. Mikhail said it might help to unravel the mystery. My father's name was known in engineering circles, although he and Mikhail had never met. After his disappearance he had become of interest to many students, including Uncle M. I was nervous, my real name had been hidden for so long, it felt wrong to be saying it out loud. Mikhail was a professor of physics and mathematics and he was convinced that my father would have left clues.

The talk went on into the night with no real conclusion, except that we knew our next destination was to be St Petersburg. Aunty K had been there once with the fair so it would not be totally strange to her. We were to stay with friends of Mikhail. They had studied together before the strike.

One of these friends, Alexander, had been part of the student demonstrations and had been discredited and sent home. Although wealthy, Alex was no lover of the establishment. His family owned a farm outside of the city. It was there we were to stay and work for a while. Our funds were very low, so it was important to earn our keep and save some money for the ongoing journey.

I had been suspicious of Mikhail at first, but both Aunty E and Aunty K seemed to be at ease with him. Aunty E was, after all, my father's sister, and would not put her brother at any risk. At times such as these, with strikes, disappearances and talks of war, it was difficult to trust anyone. Once they had gone back to Moscow, Aunty K and I had a long heartfelt talk. I told her of my fears, and she, being wise as usual, said that she thought that everything was as it should be, but of course we must still be secretive and on our guard.

Aunty E seemed much more friendly than when we had lived underground, and I too was changed. The more I thought about it, the more I came to realise that everyone had been acting in a strange manner to ensure my safety.

My mother and father must have been held in very high regard, I thought.

Chapter Fifteen

St Petersburg

When we finally left the dacha, it was with a mixture of sadness and excitement. We were taken to the station to await the St Petersburg train. Before our train was due for boarding, a troop train came through the station. It was a very long train, with many carriages filled with young men being sent to defend the borders. It made everything much more real, serious and frightening.

We waited nervously while our papers were checked, then finally we were on the train. How I longed for a settled, simple life, not knowing that things had changed forever.

We wandered through the train to find our places. Looking through the doors of the first- and second-class carriages, we could see that they were beautifully laid out with curtains, tablecloths and other finery befitting the high status of the travellers. I thought to myself, one day I would like to travel in such a manner.

We made our way to the third-class section, from where we would be making our journey. The carriage was full already and the talk was of the impending war and how it would affect everyone. Everything was rapidly changing, even including the name of the city we were going to. Always known to us as St Petersburg, it was to be renamed as Petrograd. I asked why this was, but no one seemed to know, until an old man in the corner of the carriage spoke. It was because the original name sounded too German, he said, and that was not desirable with the outbreak of war. It all suddenly became very real. Even though I had seen the troop trains, it had never felt immediate.

We huddled into our seats and I fell into a fitful sleep. The journey was to take almost two days so we needed to take all the rest we could. Aunty K was very quiet, very unlike her, so I knew she was also worried. When we started our quest life was simpler and the world seemed settled with itself. I wondered if she regretted coming with me, but if she did she said nothing.

People ate their meagre rations, sharing what they could and keeping some back for their onward journey. What scenery we did see was beautiful, through villages and some towns, where the train made the occasional stop. The carriage got more and more crowded and some of the conversations got very heated. People expressed their differing views about whose fault it was, what should happen next, who it would affect, but mainly in their mistrust of the Tsar. I whispered to Aunty K that I thought it was something to do with the assassination of the relative of the Kaiser, but that seemed to have been forgotten in the rush into open war. Aunty K said, quietly, that it would be better to stay out of the talks, so we feigned sleep on a number of occasions.

It felt a very long and uncomfortable journey, but at last we reached our destination. Following our very good directions, we duly arrived at the farm, a few kilometres outside of the city. The old couple there were very welcoming. They had learnt of our arrival from a friend who worked at the telephone exchange in the local community office. I marvelled that these machines were now operating in much of Russia, I remember how excited we all were when the first one was installed in the shipping office back in Brasov. We had no idea then how much would change during the war and in the aftermath of the uprising three years later.

We stayed at the farm for two nights and on the Sunday we were to visit the son and his wife who lived in the city itself. They were part of the intelligentsia and ruling class. I felt very much out of my depth, but Aunty K had no such problems. It amazed me how she could fit in anywhere. The family owned a carriage and two chestnut-coloured horses. On seeing them I thought of Hercules, our gentle country horse, big boned and heavy. I loved him and no other horses, however stately, would replace him in my heart. I hoped that he and Hans had safely returned to Suceava, and in many ways I wished I was there with them.

Mikhail's friend was now also a professor, in the same field. His wife, Christobel, a beautiful young woman with hair the colour of sunshine, worked with the local doctor and was well known for her good deeds in the city. Although he was from a privileged background, Alex and his wife shared a liberal attitude, hence the reason for helping Aunty K and me. I suspected that he also knew of my father. We were to stay a few days with them, and this was to include a trip around the city and an invitation to a party. It was all so exciting. We made ready for the carriage ride.

The city had many beautiful buildings with architecture the likes of which I had never seen before. The buildings in Moscow did not compare, as this city had an air of refinement about it. We travelled past rows of grand homes and palaces that lined the wide tree-lined streets until we reached the Summer Garden Park, magnificent with its shrubs and trees, the walkways and the lake. The high society of the city were out, walking or in their carriages. It was a colourful scene, spoilt only by the sense of foreboding in the air. We travelled along the banks of the Neva, where we saw the battleship *Aurora* birthed in front of the Summer Palace, and the fortress of Peter and Paul. The midday canon boomed out, giving me quite a fright. This city was the seat of government and the imperial court of the Romanovs. There were so many interesting buildings and I marvelled at the opulence on show all around us.

We were to attend a party the next evening, for which Christobel, our hostess, kindly lent Aunty K and me some suitable clothes. What an evening we had, the food, the music and the dancing, I began to feel guilty that I was enjoying myself so much. After all, this was probably the society that had sent my parents into exile. I stayed close to Aunty K and as always we were very guarded in our conversations. The amazing night ended, and I fell into a disturbed night's sleep, due more to excitement than anxiousness.

The next day we were to attend church, having not been since we had started the journey. We attended the Church of the Spilled Blood, so called because it was where a previous tsar, Alexander II, had been assassinated. The inside of the church was decorated with paintings of saints and biblical scenes on every wall and column. I'm afraid that I spent more time looking at the decorations than listening to the service. The church was a beautiful setting for a very cruel deed, and I found it hard to understand why people could be so unfeeling towards each other, but then I was very naïve in the ways of the world and politics.

One thing I did begin to see was the distinct contrast between the wealth of those in St Petersburg and the poverty of the surrounding countryside.

Chapter Sixteen

On the Farm

Back in the apartment, a very serious discussion took place. The winter was coming and that coupled with the war, which had now begun in earnest, lead to the decision that we would stay on at the farm. It would be shelter for us and help for the parents, especially as their male workers had been taken away to join the army.

There was a small house on the land where we could stay, and in return for the food and a bed, we would help with the daily chores. This was something I was much more used to, plus they had a big old farm horse who reminded me of my Hercules. I asked to be put in charge of him, to which Aunty K agreed. I think she was happy that I shared her love of horses.

There was much to do on the farm, and we returned to our little home tired but happy at the end of each day. The temperature began to drop and one day the snows came, making working life very difficult. Aunty K worked with the livestock, while my job was to see to the chickens, the vegetable garden and the old horse. I named him Baikal, after my home area, but that was just between him and me.

We did not see much of the parents, but Aunty K would let them know what we were doing, and give them the money if we sold anything. This was returned in the form of our keep and a small amount for us. It was a good arrangement and we were able to save small amounts as the weeks passed. Christmas came and the professor and his wife came to stay for the celebrations, to which we were also invited. It was a little affair, as we did not want to attract the notice of the military who were obtaining manpower and supplies from everywhere they could. The Russian army was in no way ready nor as well equipped as the German army and this was starting to show in the numbers of casualties on the battlefronts.

It was decided that we would move on to Finland, which was at that time still part of Russia, in the spring. Crossing the border would not be too much trouble, and also a new railway line had been built the year before. Now that I was 20, we decided I was old enough to go on alone. It would not be for several months but Aunty K, understandably, did not want to leave mainland Russia completely. She still had her home in Romania, to which she hoped to return.

I absolutely understood, this was my quest after all, and she had been truly wonderful travelling with me for so long. Besides, there was talk of the fair coming to St Petersburg, or should I say, Petrograd, sometime in September, and her intention was to leave with them. The winter months went slowly, the heavy snows making things difficult, and we went about our work the best we could. We were always happy to get back to our cottage for our hot soup and very comforting hot chocolate.

As spring approached, the planting of the seeds was of the greatest importance. The snows had melted but the ground was still hard, making our job almost impossible but very necessary for the next harvest. The old couple were very grateful for our help, as we were to them for the shelter and safety of the farm.

Stories had been circulating of a terrible Russian defeat in East Prussia, which made us all very afraid. Conscription had started the year before and new infirmaries had opened up in the city, so we knew that more food and equipment would be needed. We learned this information from Christobel on one of our trips up to market. Her husband had been taken to work with staff officers at the front, while she worked as a nurse at the Winter Palace Infirmary.

We did not stay long in the city, but hurried back to the farm. We realised that we would not be able to make any plans until life became more settled. It was very unlikely that the fair would come to the city now, so we went about making our life as normal as possible. The old folk were pleased that we were staying on, and the farm would continue to grow food.

It was a fraught year and on many occasions we thought that the army would appear and take over, but it was a very small farm and seemed to escape notice. Although I was disappointed, I knew that it would be unsafe to travel, and as to my quest, I had waited this long, so it was my fate to wait a little longer. Aunty K was also upset as she so wanted to return home, but we both realised that our safety lay in staying at the farm.

Some of the local girls had come to help gather in the harvest and, once done, we talked again with the old couple about leaving. Spring was to be the chosen time, so we made our plans through the winter months. Christmas came and went. The war raged on with losses and gains on each side.

Had the whole world gone mad? It certainly seemed so.

We had stopped our trips to the market and used what we produced to feed ourselves, our two new workers and the old couple. The few cattle provided milk, the chickens the eggs, and the occasional lamb satisfied our meat needs.

The old couple were becoming increasingly frail and we managed to get word to Christobel and, in turn, to Alex. It had been a difficult decision because we did not want to alert the army to the existence of the farm, but felt that he should know. Being a very resourceful man, he managed to obtain leave to come back to the city, and thence to the farm.

We were shocked when we saw him, thin and looking much older. The war, he told us, was taking a great toll on all of the men at the front, especially the infantry. Cocooned in the country, we had no idea of the conditions being endured. One of the problems was that there were not enough rifles to arm all of the men, many having to wait to use the rifles of their fallen comrades. Equipment supply was one of Alexander's responsibilities, a role that he was finding increasingly difficult.

Christobel was not able to come as she was needed at the hospital, casualty rates were increasing rapidly. I do not think that the full horror of what was happening had hit me until that moment. We did not know what to do. We desperately wanted to leave but felt we could not leave these kind people who had given us shelter for so long.

Chapter Seventeen

Another Train Journey

The decision was made for us the following month. While the land was still draped in its snowy coat, the army arrived and commandeered the farm. They put in their own people to toil the land and Aunty K and I were taken to the city to train as nurses.

The endless flow of wounded soldiers soon took up all of our time, and we did what we could to alleviate their suffering. Once we had recovered from the deep melancholy we had fallen into, we began to make plans. We had hoped to go with the steady trickle of people leaving the city, but this began to look more and more unlikely.

Winter ended and spring came into being. We had managed to save a little money from the farm which we had successfully hidden when forced to leave our sanctuary. We discovered that there was a train line to Finland and thought this could be a good way of leaving mainland Russia. Aunty K would have to come too, as going home to Romania at this time was not an option. We decided that we would leave by July, and so made our plans. We told no one, not even Christobel, who had been moved to another hospital. We thought it better that she did not know so would not be held responsible for our disappearance.

We worked hard at the hospital, making sure that we were not split up. Our chores at first were mainly domestic, washing bed linen, cleaning floors, emptying bed pans and generally assisting the more senior nurses and doctors. After we had been there some time we were trusted to change dressings and administer medicines. The stream of injured soldiers being admitted was neverending. The injuries were not just of the physical kind, although they were truly appalling, bodies shattered by bullets and shrapnel, but also the mental and emotional scars were all too evident. We were too shocked to talk about it all back in our room, having witnessed too many scenes of heartbreak.

Towards the end of June, we learned that some of the injured Finnish soldiers were to be sent home, so we volunteered to travel with them. They were to recuperate then rejoin the army once fit. It was the perfect opportunity for us as we could still feel that we were helping with the war effort. It took quite some persuading of the local authorities to let us go with the party, but eventually we got our papers. We had to leave everything behind apart from our clothes and the small amount of money we had hidden.

I asked Aunty K how she felt about this, but she assured me that it was acceptable to her. This was not the Russia that she knew, or indeed wanted to know, as rival factions were raising their very ugly heads and there was much unrest in the country. It was not just the war with the Germans. I, too, felt the same and worried for everyone I knew. Aunty K said she would try to get home to Brasov at some time, but realised that it may take many years. I felt responsible for taking her away, but she said it was her choice and it must have been written into her destiny. I loved her so much, my admiration for her growing each day.

The train was to carry 200 men, 30 guards and four nurses. The nurses were to travel in a central carriage with the medical supplies, guarded by two sentries. I had never seen weapons so close up, and I found it very frightening. Finland at that time had men fighting on both sides, hence the reason for the armed guards on the train. I found it all very difficult to understand who was fighting who, where and why. Luckily we had a certain amount of anonymity hidden behind our nurses uniforms. Our main problem was how we were to slip away once we reached Finland.

The decision to travel to Finland had been reached following a conversation with Alex and Christobel involving my name, the numbers on the back of the paintings, and the bracelet given to me by Aunty A many years before.

I did not understand any of it, except that the few trusted people we had met were working to protect me. My parents must have made a big impact on everyone, I reasoned. Aunty K seemed to understand and was still happy to travel with me, even though I knew she so desperately wanted to go home. We did not know how far the war had spread or whether Romania was involved.

The train was a troop train, and as such, not very comfortable. It was to take two days to reach our destination outside of Helsinki. The other two nurses, Livy and Riina, were originally from Finland and had followed their sweethearts when they had joined the Russian army. Finland was still part of the grand duchy of Russia so us speaking Russian there would not be unusual.

The first day, we tended to many soldiers suffering greatly with their injuries, many with gunshot wounds, frostbite, amputations, blindness, paralysis, tuberculosis, and mental and emotional trauma. I felt so sorry for them, they looked so young. Some, I think, younger than me.

We made them as comfortable as we could, changed dressings and helped with feeding when required. Once recovered, if ever recovered, they would most likely be sent back to the Eastern Front. It made me so sad, it all seemed so futile. This was so far away from the happy days we had spent with Hercules and the caravan. How would things ever be the same again?

The night hours were very disturbed, the rocking of the train seemed to affect the men even more than in the daylight. Many called out for their sweethearts and their families. My heart ached for them, and my own quest felt so unimportant. Aunty K and I did not speak of our plans, and I was sorry for involving her. My gratitude to her knew no bounds and I hoped she knew that.

The morning bought a round of visits through the crowded carriages, the changing of blood-soaked dressings and the strong hope that no one would have died in the night, so near to home. Sadly, the smell of decay pervaded the air and a strong sense of despair could be felt throughout the train.

Finally the train rolled into the station and the evacuation of the soldiers to the recuperation hospital began. We four nurses travelled with them. The hospital was out in the countryside, staffed by a number of doctors and nurses.

We asked to be redeployed to working on the land, where we felt we would be of more use. Aunty K told them of her work with horses and was immediately sent to work at the stables. After a few days she requested that I be sent to work with her and this was allowed.

We enjoyed working with the horses, but it took us away from direct contact with the soldiers and any information we may have picked up. However, we did learn that the next-door country, Sweden, was neutral, so this was where we needed to go. It would take a lot of planning, as we had very little money, nothing left to sell and no clear idea of how we would get there.

Chapter Eighteen

The Stables

The stables were part of the local barracks and the horses there were mainly the mounts of the officers. Many of the young grooms had joined the army, some as part of the Jager divisions, and some as part of the battalions of the Russian army, and been sent to the Eastern Front. The wounded soldiers on the train must have been part of these sections. They were in a very sorry state, I could not begin to imagine the horrors they had seen and endured.

We worked very hard there, as there was much to do, mucking out, grooming and feeding the horses. In one section of the yard were the heavy horses whose job it was to pull the gun carriages. I liked it there best of all as they reminded me of Hercules, and of our happy life before the war. Each night we returned tired, but content, to our quarters.

After some months there, Aunty K was approached by an older man, who looked vaguely familiar to us. He was one of the senior doctors from the hospital, whom we had seen when we first arrived with the train. It seemed to be a very serious conversation.

He was from the old aristocracy and owned, among other things, a number of thoroughbred horses, some of which had been requisitioned by the army. He was worried about what might become of them and wanted Aunty K to take charge of them. As they were part of the war effort, it should not be too difficult to get her reassigned to the new location. She had agreed, but only if I could go with her, she did not want to be split up from her "daughter". She assured him that I could also be of help.

He had been a high ranking officer during his time in the army, and was still serving his country in his efforts at the hospital. I doubted that the authorities would let us go, as we were already fulfilling the roles left vacant by those who had been sent to the front. He must, however, have put up a very good case, for some days later we were told to collect together what few belongings we had, were given new papers and told to report to the railway station.

Another train journey, we were getting quite used to them now. Fortunately it was not too far away, just a few hours. We were met at the station by an elderly man, who sadly we could not understand as he spoke to us in a strange language, but with a series of gestures and pointing, we were able to communicate. I wondered why it was different to what was spoken at the hospital and the barracks, which I took to be a mixture of Finnish and Russian. Aunty K told me that very often the landed gentry of this country were of Swedish origin, from the days when Finland was part of the Swedish Empire. It was all very confusing, and I felt sorry for the country, being taken over so many times, and not belonging to itself, and having more languages to learn.

The old man had a kindly manner, and before long our carriage arrived at the farm. It stretched for as far as you could see, with a large house and stable area at the heart of it. This was indeed the home of a very wealthy person. Aunty K, as usual, took it all in her stride.

We were shown to an outhouse building, inside which was a cosy cabin. We left our few belongings there and were taken to the kitchens to meet the rest of the staff, and for some welcome hot food. At first there was some resistance in befriending us as we were Russian and were met with some suspicion. The household were from Finnish peasantry, but spoke some Swedish in deference to the Master. There was a good atmosphere, so we started to relax. We learned two things, one was that the Doctor and his wife were held in high regard, and two, that the old housekeeper, wife of the old man, was originally from Russia and so was able to speak to us in simple words, from a language she had almost forgotten.

Aunty K told her of our intention to learn the local languages, and that we would be grateful for any help. Each day we learnt more and more, speaking Russian only in our cabin. The stables were at the side of the house, across a large courtyard. A young boy of about 15 was working there, and I think he was pleased to see us, to share the workload. There were about 20 horses in the paddock, and at least 10 more in the stables area.

There were several pregnant mares and two highly spirited stallions. To my delight, there were also four heavy horses. I immediately asked to tend to them.

It was hoped that the Doctor would come home in the next few days, then we would have a better idea of what he wanted with us. Aunty K, with her confidence, friendliness and knowledge, had soon won over the staff. With plenty of help, mainly of the housekeeper, we had begun to learn some of the languages.

The staff consisted of the old lady Olga, her husband Frederik, the stable boy Erik and his mother Agnis, and the two older men who worked in the fields. The horses had been reasonably well looked after, the young boy had done his best. Aunty K took charge, making sure that Erik still worked with her. She taught him many new things. His mother helped in the kitchens and with the general household chores. I helped with the horses on occasion, but the heavy horses were my responsibility. I would not have believed that I would have loved these creatures so much, and I knew it was all because of patient Hercules.

The Doctor came and went several times, his wife only once, as she was needed at the hospital. We worked very hard; the weeks became months and before we knew it, we had been there a year. We had heard alarming stories of a civil war raging in Russia and were so glad that we were not there, although we worried terribly for the people we knew. I also worried for Aunty K. Her chances of returning home were becoming more and more remote.

Finland, thankfully, had not yet been fully involved in the internal troubles, although there had been some isolated outbreaks of fighting. The war was still going on. We realised it was all the more important for us to move on before the borders were closed. Sweden was our goal, and this was why we had been learning Swedish as well as Finnish. We had to make our plans in secret, as we could not involve anyone else in them. It was all so unsafe for us all.

Agnis had relatives in Sweden, of whom she spoke most fondly. We listened carefully to her conversations, picking up any clues that we could. The border was about three days' journey, through territory that we did not know. Our move would have to be in late summer, as the harvest would need to be gathered before then, and we would all be needed to help, including my four heavy horses.

We had all learned to live together, carrying out our individual tasks and working closely when necessary. Aunty K helped when she could, but mostly she and Erik were taken up with seeing to and exercising the horses. They were magnificent beasts, with their sleek coats and proud bearing. Occasionally army officers would come to choose their mounts, fortunately paying no attention to us, the peasant stock running the farm. We in turn did nothing to attract their attention.

Chapter Nineteen

Road to Sweden

We were still working on our plan to move on to Sweden. I had another birthday and was now 22, although my papers stated that I was 19. We celebrated quietly in the cabin, speaking in our mother tongue. I found it a strain having to learn new languages, and was glad to relax into our true selves in the evenings. Even if we were overhead, no one except the old housekeeper could understand, and she never ventured out of the main house.

Once a week we all had a meal together in the farmhouse to make the work plans for the following week, the old man and his wife being in charge when the Master was not there. They had done their jobs well for many years. Cocooned in this little world, it was easy to forget that there was a bitter war being fought just outside its borders.

Winter came once again, it was very cold, and I thought of the times around the lake when I was growing up. Aunty K did not speak much about her home in Romania, I felt very sorry that I had taken her away from it, and now she could not get home. I caught glimpses of the wistful look in her eyes and my heart ached for her. When she did talk, it was about the horses and how she loved working with them.

Christmas was approaching, and the homecoming of the Doctor and his wife. We were all invited to the celebrations and it was good to get away from all of the hard work for a few hours. We knew that we must be careful not to give away any of our plans. Aunty K had been teaching Erik many new skills and he was an able student. I faded into the background so was of little interest to anyone. This, of course, was a deliberate ploy, so that we would not come to the attention of the visiting army personnel. We planned to leave a letter for the Doctor, but that was for later, now all we needed to do was survive the winter.

We learnt all we could from Agnis, about her relatives and travel around Sweden. All information was gathered slowly and carefully so as not to alert anyone of our purpose. It would have been very easy to stay with these very kind people, but we had come so far and given up too much to end our quest now. We were making progress learning the languages, albeit on a very simple level.

The winter seemed so long, but at last the thaw set in and the spring buds began to sprout. It really had to be now, or we would never go. There was unrest around the countryside, and we learnt that the Tsar and his family were under house arrest. We were shocked, as now there was also civil war raging in Russia. How long before it spread to Finland?

Fate helped us once again, as we were asked to go into Helsinki to assist in the sale of some of the horses. Aunty K was to take part in the negotiations. I begged to go along too. This could act as a practice run for our leaving. Erik was to accompany us. It was a nice change to go into the city, to our meeting point at the railway station. It was to be my task to find out about trains to Sweden. Aunty K, Erik and the Doctor were to negotiate the sale.

Sadly there were no passenger trains to Sweden, but I did hear of a border crossing up north, at a place called Tornio.

On meeting up again with Aunty K, I could see she was accompanied by a tall man with military bearing. Erik had been sent to fetch the Doctor. The five of us met up at the nearby train yards, where the deal was struck. Twenty five of the horses, one stallion and two of the heavy horses were to be sold. All pregnant mares, the yearlings and one stallion were to stay at the farm, at least for now. This suited our purpose as it would be much less for Erik to deal with once we were gone.

While at the station, I had heard another piece of news that I was sure would be of benefit to us. There was to be an exchange of invalided foreign soldiers at a crossing point between Finland and Sweden, and Red Cross nurses were needed to travel with them. It had been instigated by a nurse named Elsa Brandstrom, a woman of some repute. We would need to persuade the Doctor to let us go. There would be much less work at the farm from now on.

I felt so sorry for him, because we all knew that if he did not agree to the sale, the army would just take the horses. At least he would make a little money, but nowhere near their actual worth. War was such an evil thing, it was not just the soldiers who were involved. I was learning so much about life, and a lot of it I did not like. It had turned out to be a very strange day, but there was at least some hope for Aunty K and me in realising our plans to move on.

The Doctor sadly and reluctantly agreed to everything. All that his family had built up was being taken away. The quartermaster went to make the arrangements. Aunty K later spoke to the Doctor in regard to us, as there was no longer a need for us to be at the farm, we were just extra mouths to feed. He said that he would release us from any obligations, as long as Aunty K oversaw the sale and movement of the horses. The troop trains were due to start in three weeks' time, and he would ensure that we were on one. We were so grateful to him. Erik said nothing, but I could see he was upset, so many things were going to change.

We travelled back to the farm, each deep in our own thoughts, to await the detachment of soldiers sent to take charge of the horses.

Chapter Twenty

Tornio

News of our leaving was met with some dismay. We had become like a family, with mutual respect for one another, even though we came from many different places. We said we felt it was time to move on, and that we never stayed anywhere too long. We said we were going back to being Red Cross volunteers, dealing with the repatriation of prisoners of war. We had arrived there from a troop train in the beginning, so it felt only right to be leaving the same way.

The soldiers arrived to take the horses. We were so sorry that these beautiful animals were having to go into a war zone, it was so sad. This war, although we had no direct experience of it, seemed to be going on forever. Stories we heard were beyond imagination. The few horses that were left would be tended to by Erik. He had learnt much from Aunty K. Fortunately he looked much younger than his age and so avoided conscription. The older men stayed out of sight in the fields, so the farm appeared to be looked after only by the old folk, Agnis and Erik. We, by then, had our new papers to join the Red Cross nurses and would leave the following week.

We packed then had our last evening meal with our "family" and said our goodbyes, ready for our move the next morning. There were many tears as we wished each other luck and future happiness. The old man took us back to Helsinki. It seemed like so little time since we had arrived with him, yet it was over a year.

We met up with the other volunteers at the station and were told what our roles were to be in the evacuation. Injured German prisoner of war soldiers were to be exchanged for Russian soldiers. The head nurse was a pupil of Elsa Brandstrom, another fascinating woman who cared very much for the welfare of her charges, regardless of their nationality. Many people were caught up in a war that was none of their making, and where they had no wish to be. I liked the sound of her, she was an Aunty K sort of person.

We were allotted our carriage for the two-day journey. Some of the other volunteers seemed very young and I wondered how they would cope with everything. I was not much older, but I had been on a hospital train before. Even so, I was not prepared for what I saw.

The exchanged prisoners of war were in a very sorry state, some better than others. What struck me the most was how young they were, some barely more than teenagers. Even though we knew of the fighting, we had not experienced it first-hand. They reminded me of the fishermen from home, the young men from the shipping office, the field workers from the farms, the only difference being that these boys were German. There was no strutting arrogance, just frightened, hurt young men wanting to go home and be with their families. A feeling I knew well.

The train jolted and our journey began. I thought about the train coming from the other direction, full of Russian soldiers, probably of similar ages to these boys, their lives forever changed. There was not too much to do, mainly changing dressings and sharing out what little food there was, and giving them water. I hoped that our Russian soldiers would be treated with the same kindnesses. It was all too awful.

Aunty K and I decided to converse in Romanian, in the hope that no one could understand us. It was mostly a quiet journey, this was not the place for frivolity, although there was time to exchange smiles. The train made very slow progress as we headed north. Some of the soldiers had come from the camps in the Siberia region and I longed to talk to them about the lake and my home. This, of course, was not possible, and a dangerous thing to do. The war was still going on, and these men were our enemies. They were little more than boys. Many on both sides had been killed and their replacements were getting younger and younger.

Finally we came to Tornio, where the border crossing into the Swedish town of Haparanda was situated. The mood of the train lifted as the men knew that once they were in Sweden it was neutral ground and they would be on their way to Germany. I wondered how many of them would have to carry on fighting once they had recovered. This was also a time of silent celebration for me and Aunty K as we would be one step nearer to our goal.

We were a long time at the border while all the paperwork checks were made, but finally we moved on to Harpandra and freedom. There were a number of Red Cross volunteers, like us, waiting to transfer the men to the mobile hospital used to carry out health checks before their movement through Sweden.

The incoming train carrying the Russian soldiers had not yet arrived, and we were told to go to the Russian section of the holding camp to await our return orders. It was time to seize our chance and leave, we would never have a better opportunity. At the back of the camp was a small farm and kitchens, supplying the food needs. We presented ourselves, and speaking in our best Swedish, said we were volunteers come to help with the land work. When asked where we were from, we mentioned the village where the relatives of Agnis were from, a place we knew of well from her many stories.

We were welcomed and soon set to work. We felt that we were still doing something for the war effort, soothing our feelings of guilt about leaving Finland and our last links with our homeland. Our Red Cross vestments exchanged for peasant clothes and headscarves, and with our dirty faces we looked no different than the other farm workers. We worked hard and kept to ourselves.

The Russian train arrived but we stayed away from the main camp. It was time to make new plans for our onward journey.

Part Three
"Life in a new Age"

Chapter Twenty One

At the Camp

All who arrived in the camp were given a medical check, as there had been stories of an influenza-like condition among the soldiers. Once given the all clear, they were given a bowl of thick warm soup. There were so many broken men, my heart went out to them. Broken not just in body, but in spirit too. How would anyone recover from this?

Aunty K and I worked very hard alongside the other volunteers in exchange for food and a bed. A number of trains from both sides arrived, until one day they just stopped, leaving behind only the men who were too sick to travel. I did not like to think what would happen to them.

The trains were due to start arriving again the following month. We knew we must leave, and perhaps in the confusion of the next arrivals we could slip quietly away. Seeing all these people who would never see their families again made me even more determined. We had no idea of a route as we had no access to maps, we could only rely on the chatter around us.

Many of the volunteers were Swedish and would talk of their homes. Sweden sounded a lot like Romania with its many farms dotted across the landscape. We were confident that we would find work once we were on the road. News came of the next arrivals, so we readied our plan. Aunty K was asked to go into the town for supplies. She returned with the information we needed. We decided to move on the day of the arrival of the first train, and that we would head for a place named Karlstad. We had heard it was rural, with a large lake, and more importantly it was on the route to Gothenburg, a large exit port.

The train arrived and we helped with the transfer of the soldiers to the camp. After the meals were served, it was time to go. We had hidden our belongings at a pick-up point the previous night to avert any suspicion. It was a difficult day full of indecision, as we were torn between helping in the camp and carrying on with our quest. We were, of course, free to leave at any time as we were volunteers, but we still felt conflicted. We told the others we had heard news of family illness and so must leave.

We left as twilight fell and decided to stay in a nearby wooded area until dark. We would travel by moonlight. For the first few days we only travelled at night for a few hours then settled into a makeshift shelter for sleep. We no longer had the lightness of spirit that we had when first leaving Romania, my dreams of finding my parents growing ever dimmer. We had seen so much over the past three years, images that would never leave us.

Once we had some distance from the camp, we travelled by day. The few supplies we had brought were running out, so we needed to find work and make some money.

We foraged for what we could find in the forests, but that soon lost its appeal for me as I longed for a big bowl of hot soup and a wedge of crusty bread. We were headed south-west, passing through large areas of farmland.

One day we passed a field with a lone horse in it, galloping around in a frenzy. Rearing and snorting, he was in a very bad humour. Aunty K went to the fence and gently and quietly started to call him. He eyed her with great suspicion, but slowly started to calm and eventually walked over to her. She stroked his head, and still speaking very soothingly to him, she climbed over the fence. I knew that she was good with horses, but I had never seen anything like this.

She patted him down then announced that she knew what the problem was. The poor creature was full of brambles, which had become entangled in his mane and tail. His constant thrashing about had dug the brambles into his coat and the sores there had become infected.

Using her headscarf and the water from the small stream nearby, she bathed him and removed what brambles she could, all of the time talking to him in her low gentle voice. She stroked him until he became completely calm. Unbeknown to us, a young boy had been watching, and had gone to fetch the owner of the horse, who appeared by my side. He was a man of middle age who, like me, stood in awe, silently watching Aunty K weave her magic.

Once Aunty K had tended to him, the beautiful animal lay his head on her neck. It was amazing to watch. The man called out to her, and she and the horse came over to the fence. No one had been able to get near the poor animal to help him. She said that she knew he would not hurt her. She loved horses, and they her. The grateful man insisted we come to his farm for some food.

We were more than happy. He lived with his wife, a boy and two girls. They were so welcoming and listened avidly as he told them what he had seen. Naturally, they were curious about where we had come from, so we were as truthful as we could be, saying we were on our way to Gothenburg, looking for family. They knew little of the war and we did not want to tell them of all the suffering we had seen. They offered us a bed for the night, which we gratefully accepted. The farmer, Sven, asked if we would stay a few days to oversee the recovery of the horse. We agreed and said that we would work around the farm for our food and lodgings. Aunty K continued to tend to the horse's wounds. It was not a large farm and the loss of the horse would have caused much hardship. The wife was Anna, the boy

Niclaus, and the two girls Christina and Freya. It was a happy home and we would eventually stay on for several months.

Chapter Twenty Two

On to Karlstad

The time passed peacefully, and we worked hard in our various roles. There was an outhouse which was converted into our living quarters. Sven, Aunty K and Niclaus looked after the animals while I helped in the fields with the two girls. Anna ran the household, and was an exceptionally good cook. This was a contented home, untouched by the war and the terrible disease that followed it.

We, talked long into the night about all that had happened, what we had seen, and what we needed to do next. We needed more information, but how to get it? We had come to Sweden following our talks with Aunty E and Mikhail. It had been mentioned that many academics had fled to Sweden and from there to America. I had heard of America as it was one of the places served by the shipping office in Brasov. I also knew it was a very large country, so to find two people seemed impossible. One thing in our favour was that immigrants from different countries tended to settle in known areas, building their communities anew. We hoped that once we got to Gothenburg we would find more information. Hopefully someone would know something, but I had my doubts as it had been more than 15 years, but Aunty K was optimistic as always.

Another winter was approaching so it suited everyone for us to stay and help out on the farm. The family were poor, so growing and harvesting the vegetables and animal feed was very important, and with this we were able to help. The horse fully recovered. Living with these kind people, and conversing with them each day, had helped us improve our Swedish. For the first time in a very long time, I began to feel safe and settled.

Karlstad was many hours travel from where we were, but we learnt that come spring there was a large produce market to which we, Sven and Niclaus would travel. The thought of this made the winter easier to bear as we went about our daily tasks. I enjoyed talking with the children and wondered if perhaps I should think of teaching as a vocation. I found great satisfaction in passing on knowledge. Another Christmas tide was celebrated, and plans made for the coming year. I was fascinated by how the festivities were celebrated in the different countries we had visited. We loved being with the family, but we knew we had to move on, and most importantly, make some money.

Spring arrived and there was much activity making ready for the market. This was where we were to leave them and continue our travels. It was sad wishing Anna and the girls goodbye, but they understood and wished us luck and happiness. The day of the market came, the cart filled with the early produce to sell, and so we set off in the dark hours before dawn. Aunty K walked up front with the horse some of the way, and we took it in turns to walk or ride on the cart. It was a long way, but we arrived at a goodly hour, in time to set up a stall and begin selling what we had brought. I began to enjoy myself, it felt good to do something normal and fun, after all of the horror we had seen.

Sven introduced Aunty K to some of the other farmers, telling them of how she had saved his horse. All too soon the day was over and it was time to part. Sven said that we should take a little of the money, as a thank you for everything. We did not like to, as he needed all he could get for his family. He was insistent, so we accepted just enough for food and lodgings for the night. It would give us chance to look for other employment. It was a sad parting, but we all knew it was something we had to do.

We fell gratefully into our beds in a small lodging house off the square. Fed, warm and safe, we talked a little then fell into an exhausted sleep. The next day was for exploring. Outside of the town limits there was a large lake. My heart soared when I saw it, it was just like the one at home. I thought of Aunty A, Tomas, of the fishermen and the people in the village, and I felt deeply homesick. I sat on the shoreline and cried. The tears were for everything we had seen and done, some things sad, some joyful, but mostly for the time passing us by and the home I missed. This quest had seemed so important at the beginning, nothing else had mattered, but now I was not so sure. I looked over at Aunty K, and although I knew she carried the same sadness, she did not speak of it. As always, she busied herself, planning our next move and the huge task of getting us some money.

I saw her talking to a group of gentlemen and from the smile on her face I knew she must have gained us some employment. It was not employment, it was actually a means of transport to our next destination. One of the men owned a car. The only vehicles I had seen were trains or horse drawn carriages. It seems that the man was a wealthy land owner and was visiting friends. He was of a similar age to Aunty K, and on meeting him, I could see that he was attracted to her. This time I was introduced as her niece. He had said he would take us to Vänersborg, from there we could continue into Gothenburg.

He was leaving the next morning and an agreement was made to meet us near the market entrance. We spent a happy but restless night, and early the next day we were at the meeting place. Aunty K had offered him what little money we had, but he declined, saying he would enjoy having company on the return journey. He arrived in a strange-looking vehicle that spluttered and coughed as it came to a stop, but looked beautiful. Sleek, with green shiny paintwork, brass trim, spoked wheels and black leather seats, the car had a fold-down roof and our luggage was put into a large box attached to the back of it. I sat on the back seat, with Aunty K riding up front. I had never seen such a thing, it was magnificent. We started off, the wind in our hair as this loud purring beast rode off through the lanes. The man was called Carl Gustav. I could not hear their conversation, but was content to sit back and enjoy the scenery passing by. It felt so fast, but I did not feel unsafe. Many hours would pass until we finally reached our destination.

Chapter Twenty Three

Gothenburg

The town was situated at the southernmost tip of the large lake that we had seen in Karlstad. The journey in the car was certainly a most strange experience and we saw very few other vehicles on the road to Vänersborg. Everything was changing so fast in this new century – electric trams, ships with turbines, and now cars. This one was apparently called a Scania-Vabis Phaeton, a very grand name I thought, but then it was a very grand car.

Aunty K and the man, Carl, chatted for the whole journey. The countryside was beautiful as we travelled down the side of the lake. An overwhelming feeling of homesickness hit me again, my thoughts and feelings were in such conflict. Part of me really longed for the settled days at the lakeside with Tomas before all of this had begun. I missed the happy days in Romania with Aunty K, Hans, and my big patient friend Hercules. What had become of everyone, had they survived the war? With my whole being, I hoped so. And what of my parents, the whole reason for this search. Were they still alive? Would they remember me? where were they? There were so many questions. All of this went through my head as we travelled down the winding roads to our destination.

Carl was a gentleman of obvious wealth, that was plain to see, but he had a kindly, gentle manner. He said he would like to take us to his home for some food, before taking us to the town. We readily agreed, this would help our very limited budget, and also we enjoyed his company. He and Aunty K had struck up a friendship, even in the short journey time, and I was glad. I wondered if anything would come of it. I hoped so, I loved her dearly and it was time she had some happiness of her own. Uncle Stephan would always be in her heart, but she should not be alone for the rest of her life. She was the most amazing person I knew.

We turned into a long drive, at the top of which was a large house. I had never seen a place so grand. Over the meal he told us more about his life and work. He too had been married, but had lost his wife to the sweating sickness some years earlier. He lived in the house with his housekeeper, a maid and two men who worked around the estate. His family were part owners of the large Olidan Hydroelectric Power Station, built some years earlier in 1910, supplying electricity to the railways and industry. Also, he had personally been involved in the planning and construction of a series of lift locks linking Lake Vanern to the North Sea.

We were fascinated. He told us about the Trollhättan waterfalls and how the boats travelling along the river Göta älv would use the locks to adjust for the height differences in the river. This would allow them to continue on to Gothenburg and the sea. No wonder Aunty K liked him, they were kindred spirits, both with such interesting stories to tell.

We were invited to stay for a few days, being fed the best food we had tasted. Carl was the perfect host and it was becoming more and more obvious that there was an attraction between him and Aunty K. He went about his daily work while we rested and enjoyed the luxury of his home and the surrounding countryside. He said he would get us passage on one of the small boats.

On the third evening he informed us that he had managed to book a berth on a cargo ship heading to Gothenburg, and from there we would be able to book passage to America. The next day he took us to board the ship. He had seen to all of the arrangements, we were so grateful. Since we had been in Sweden we had been shown nothing but kindness. It was an emotional farewell, but somehow I doubted it was the last that he and Aunty K would see of each other.

We were allowed on deck to watch the ship make its way through the lock system. The river level dropped 32 metres. It was fascinating, but also a little frightening. We could see the magnificent Trollhättan Falls and the electric plant. All too quickly the spectacle was over, and we were on our way to the coast. We awoke to the sights and sounds of the busy port. Once docked, we thanked the captain and went on our way.

The city was so large and noisy with many people rushing by. I found it really intimidating. Aunty K said that this was how the American cities would be and I would have to learn to cope with it. For all that I had seen and done I was still rather naïve, but I would have to learn quickly if I was to survive the journey ahead.

Chapter Twenty Four

Passage to America

We soon found lodgings, something at which we were now very adept. Once rested, our most important task was to find some paid work. The war had been over for some time and life was beginning to return to some normality, although there were still huge changes taking place in some countries.

It had already been decided that I would be going on alone, so it was mainly up to me to earn the fare. I decided to start at the Swedish American Line offices as I had some experience in shipping, having worked in Brasov. Aunty K would try at the produce market. I went to the dockside office and spoke with various people until I was at last able to speak with the chief clerk. A young man, a few years older than me, listened while I told him of my experience. He appeared to be impressed, particularly as I could communicate in four different languages. As yet I spoke little English, but I assured him that I was a very fast learner. I had also worked for several years in Brasov so was aware of shipping terms. I told him truthfully of our adventures since leaving Romania, but kept my Russian background deliberately vague.

He listened patiently, then said to return the next day to speak with the shipping officer in charge of staff. I returned to the market feeling hopeful. Aunty K had also managed to get some work on one of the stalls. She was very knowledgeable, and her calm manner made her good with dealing with suppliers and customers. She laughed as she told me it was much like dealing with the horses. I laughed too and told her that I was hopeful about the work in the office.

I presented myself the next day and was taken to see three people in a small room. Aunty K had said this might happen and to remain as calm as possible. I did my best to relax. I told them that I had lived in Romania as a very young child, that I did not know my parents, and I had lived there until my late teen years. I spoke of Aunty K, and of our role as nurses which had occurred as we had been visiting a cousin in Moscow at the outbreak of the war. I told them of our work on the various farms, but mainly I told them of my work in the Brasov shipping office. I said that I realised that things would be greatly changed, but that I had always been interested in learning new skills. I could see a nodding of heads and that made me feel more confident. They asked me a lot of questions.

I was asked to wait in the reception room while they made their decision. It felt a very long time, but eventually the clerk came to tell me yes, and that I was to see the office manager about starting times and office protocol. She was a woman in her thirties, very efficient and friendly, I liked her. She told me to report the next day. I was so pleased that I rushed to the market to tell Aunty K.

At last our lives seemed to be more settled and we could now earn some money to enable us to carry out our future plans. The heavy atmosphere of the previous years had lifted, and life was starting anew. We had a room in a boarding house near the centre. It was very sparse, but comfortable, large enough for two beds and a cooking and sitting area. The toilet facilities were down the corridor, but fortunately there were not too many people sharing. It was a new decade and the horrors of the last one were slowly being pushed into the background.

Aunty K would walk to work, while I travelled on one of the newly electrified trams. I was put to work in the sorting section where the applications for passage were made. There were so many people, from so many different nations, wanting to restart their lives. Some had letters of invitation from relatives already settled in America, and some offers of employment. These were given priority. I thought about what I would do once I arrived there. This, of course, was for the future. I had not mentioned my plans to anyone.

The ships filled up and I watched as many families left to make a new life far over the sea. The flow of emigration did slow down as conditions in the various home countries improved. I decided that I would stay for a year, making proper plans for the move. It was a leap of faith going to America but from all that I knew it would have been the logical step for my parents to have made.

Aunty K and I kept much to ourselves and blended into Swedish life as if we had been born to it. I enjoyed my time in the office and worked hard at learning English with anyone willing to teach me. We spoke Swedish at home, our Romanian and Russian almost forgotten. We had lived on our wits for so long now it was second nature.

The summer passed, the autumn trees shed their leaves and suddenly it was winter again. We celebrated Christmas the best we could, joining in when invited. We did not want to appear too aloof. My colleagues were good people, but after my experience with Natalya and Yana I did not want to become too close to anyone. Besides, I knew I would be moving on. I did, however, like one of the girls, Hannah, we were the same age and enjoyed similar things. We liked to laugh together, and spent time with each other whenever we could.

Aunty K and I talked often about the future and how she was not going to come any further with me. I knew that she missed her own life, and after all, this was my quest. I was extremely grateful to her for coming so far. It was a crossroads for me too. The step, once taken, was most likely never to be reversed.

Carl Gustav had come to visit a number times from his home at Vänersborg, and I realised that they had been in communication with each other and had become very fond of each other. I was so happy for her and was not the least surprised when he asked her to marry him. She said yes, which confirmed that our lives were definitely set on different paths.. Should I ever come back, I would know where to find her.

She made the most beautiful May bride, and the following day I boarded the *SS Drottningholm*, bound for America.

Chapter Twenty Five

The SS Drottningholm

I saved what money I could to pay for passage on the ship. I had originally planned to try for employment at the American end of the Shipping Company before I left Sweden, but that would have meant telling them of my plans so for now I decided to worry about that on arrival. First there would be the main obstacle of Ellis Island and the immigration process, and that would certainly be enough to worry about.

Before I left, we had written to Uncle Mikhail at the university, but as yet had not received a reply. We worried for him and Aunty E. From what news we had heard, it seemed that Russia was in a state of total upheaval. Very selfishly, I was glad we were not there.

When I had announced my intention to leave the office, I was surprised to find that Hannah intended to go too. We had never discussed emigration. We decided to travel together and so were able to afford a small second-class cabin. It would make life so much easier than travelling in steerage. As always, I would have to be on my guard, but I had played the role of Swedish Anna for so long now it came easily to me.

The day of the boarding was a strange one, a mixture of extreme sadness at leaving Aunty K and extreme excitement at what lay ahead. I owed her so much, I was so glad that she and Carl had each other, but nothing I could say would ever express my gratitude to her. She was the most amazing person I had ever met, something that I had thought on many occasions.

Hannah was waiting at the Stigbergskajen quay with so much luggage. I had very little, just the essentials. We walked slowly to the gangplank, and at the top, turned for one last look at Sweden, then headed down into the bowels of the ship to find our cabin. It was very small, but enough room for the two of us. I worried that we would not get on, as we did not really know each other, but my fears were unfounded. We quickly became like sisters.

We had said we would not go back outside until we reached open water, but when the ship's horn sounded we, like the other passengers, rushed up on deck to catch our last glimpse of the people waving goodbye, the city, and our previous life.

The ship slipped quietly out of the harbour, past the old fortress and out to the open sea. Aunty K had not come to the dock as we had said our goodbyes that morning. It had been such a sad affair, but we knew that our destinies lay in different directions. She now had her new life with Carl Gustav. I would write to her once I had settled somewhere. I would now have to learn to live on my wits, but I was from a long line of strong, resourceful women and had been taught well. My resolve had weakened that day as I did not want to leave Aunty K, but she reminded me that I had waited so long for this opportunity. With her soothing words I began to believe in myself.

The day before I left, we received a letter from Aunty E saying that they had survived the war, but that things were greatly changed, and Moscow was no longer a happy place to be. I could not imagine what they had been through.

Hannah and I soon settled into ship life, and were luckier than most as we had a cabin to return to at night. Our days were spent out on deck, apart from the day of the storm, when the ship was tossed about like a toy. I think that everyone was seasick that day. I felt sorry for the families in steerage, they must have had a dreadful time.

The sun finally came out again and we went back to taking our strolls around the deck, talking to the other passengers, trying to learn what English we could. I had decided to keep a diary, which I filled in each night before bed. Hannah was good company. She had relatives in Chicago and invited me to travel with her and meet her family. I was pleased as it would help me with my plans, and also I would have an address to give on landing.

Each evening we would stroll around the deck, watching the sun go down, knowing that somewhere to the west lay America and the start of our new lives. By day we would play some of the deck games, but mostly we sat on our deckchairs enjoying the sunshine. I became aware of a man watching us and the old feelings of fear started to return. I said nothing to Hannah, who was thankfully unaware. I thought about all that had happened in the recent past and wondered if I was just overreacting. Why would they come for us now?

It must have been the letter, the one sent to Aunty E and Uncle M. Had it been intercepted by agents looking for clues about my father? Surely not, after this long time. It had been so many years, another lifetime away. I could not believe it and yet my feelings told me it was so. Hannah sensed a change in me, but I said I was just nervous after the storm. I resolved to be very careful, especially now as I felt I was nearing the end of my quest. I made sure I was never on my own, Hannah and I joined in with more of the onboard activities.

How could this man know about me? It seemed impossible but of course in this new decade communications were so much faster, with telephones, telegrams and the telegraph machines. Countries had their spies everywhere. The man also watched some of the other women of my age group and it occurred to me that he did not really know who he was looking for, perhaps only having a vague description. I was now 23 and not the same shy teenager I had been on leaving Russia. I told myself to relax and enjoy the time left on the voyage.

The crossing would be coming to an end in two days, then once through customs and immigration it would be on to Chicago. My passport had been made out in the name of Anna Neilsson, thanks to the help of Carl

Gustav, so I did not foresee any problems once we landed.

One morning we started to see hazy outlines in the distance and an announcement was made to make ready for landing. It would take several hours, so once packed we stood out on deck with many others, watching the skyline of New York appear. We passed the Statue of Liberty that had been all people talked of for days, then the ship began its docking manoeuvres at the quayside.

All first- and second-class passengers were interviewed onboard the ship as to their plans, and so we were spared the clearance centre ordeal. Medical checks were carried out, and once the authorities were satisfied that we were of no risk to America we were allowed to disembark.

This was not the case for the poor people in steerage, who were to be taken by small boat to the Ellis Island centre just off the shore. The excitement and trepidation was tangible as the people flowed like a river down the gangplanks and onto the boats, to await the health and papers checks at the end of their journey.

Hannah and I stuck together as if some invisible force had bound us into one being, and were glad when we were clear of the ship. Her letter of invitation had stated only her, but she said that I was her cousin. From our chats together, I was able to answer questions about her family, and so it had been of great relief when our passports were authorised, and we stepped out onto American soil.

Chapter Twenty Six

New York

During our last couple of days on the ship I had thought much about what to do next. Hannah had kindly invited me to travel with her to Chicago, but I had thought more about it and decided to stay in New York. I had enjoyed her company, but I knew I needed to make my own plans. We would, however, stay in touch.

The area we had docked in was called Manhattan, and was like nothing I had ever encountered. It was incredibly busy, so many people, cars, buses, but still some horse and carts. It was so intimidating, and even though Aunty K had warned me of this, I was not really prepared for what I saw.

Hannah and I made our way to the main railway station, called the Grand Central Station. What a place, it certainly suited its name. There was a large booking hall, where the light rays from the high ceilings made patterns on the floor. There were ramps and elevators, ticket booths, a large information desk and baggage areas, and a big brass clock with four faces facing each main point of the compass. The whole place was lit by globe-shaped chandeliers adorned with electric bulbs. It was certainly an amazing sight, topped off by a beautiful vaulted ceiling, turquoise and gold, depicting the stars of the heavens. All in a railway station. I had never seen anything like it. There was a waiting room specifically for women, with the most beautiful oak floor, a beauty salon, and even telephones for anyone to use. Around the area there were brochures for new arrivals with accommodation addresses. I put one of them into my bag. We spent so long admiring the beautiful building that Hannah almost missed her train.

We said a fond farewell and wished each other every happiness, and with a wave she was off to her new life. Carl Gustav had kindly given me some money, for which I was extremely grateful, it would help with my rent for several weeks. I studied the brochures then spent the next hours looking for suitable lodgings. There were several locations to look at, tenements in what was called the Lower East Side of Manhattan. Some looked very drab and I could not see myself living in such places. I began to feel downhearted, when I at last turned into a pleasant tree-lined street, where the buildings had been dressed up with fancy facades. There were stores on the ground-floor levels, and good sturdy-looking fire escapes on the fronts of the buildings. I found the right address and was shown to a small but clean room, divided into various sections. I liked it, it had everything I needed, with a bedroom, small sitting area, kitchen and bathroom. I paid a month's rent and unpacked the few things I had brought. I was to learn later that the room was in the German area of the city, where there were many tailors and seamstresses.

I intended to seek employment at the shipping office, so it was vital that I continued to learn English whenever I could. There were so many life lessons to learn, but Aunty K had taught me well. After a short rest, I went to buy some of the items that I needed immediately, such as food, some pans and bed linen. My purchases acquired, I stayed in for the rest of the day, reflecting on what had happened so far and settling into my new home.

Early the next day I went back to the shipping office to register for some work. They took my name and my details, then asked me to wait in an outer office.

A rather officious man came out to see me an hour later, questioning me on everything. I told him of my experience working in the Gothenburg office and that I could type and use the telephones and speak different languages to varying degrees. He asked about my life prior to Gothenburg, so I told him about my time as a Red Cross volunteer at the recuperation hospitals and the troop trains. I became upset remembering the awful things I had seen during the war, and explained that now I had come to America to start a new life.

I told him that I was, to my knowledge, an orphan, and that my Aunty K, my previous travelling companion, had married and it was she and her husband who had sponsored my passage to America. I left out the Russian and Romanian parts of my life as I felt it would complicate matters. Besides the obvious risks of revealing all my secrets, the Romanian part of my life was by far the happiest and I wanted my memories of that time to be untainted by the dreadful events that followed. Apart from the questions he said very little, then asked me to await a decision.

It felt a very long time, the office clock ticking loudly in my ears. At last he came back and informed me that there were no suitable vacancies at present, but they would keep my details on file. I was dreadfully disappointed, but determined not to let it upset me too much. I had coped with far worse than that. Besides, it was a large city with lots of potential opportunities.

I went back into the heart of the city, and saw there a large department shop that reminded me of the one in

Moscow. I went in, and wondered if it too had a fountain and ice creams. What a place, crammed full of counters selling everything you could imagine. There were many young people working as assistants. Perhaps I could get some employment here. I asked one of the older-looking ladies, who sent me to see her supervisor on one of the higher floors. A man called me into his office, and as in the shipping office, I told him my story thus far. This time I was more successful and told to report the next day. I would at first be working in the storerooms then later I would be taught to serve at the counters on the shop floor.

It was very exciting. The next day I promptly arrived and was taken to an area where another girl of my age group, Alice, was working. She too was also originally from Sweden from a small village on the southern coast, near to Karlshamn. She was friendly and introduced me to some of the other girls. We would talk together during our short breaks. The days were long and, as winter approached, increasingly dark in the mornings and evenings when travelling to work. I was always glad to reach my cosy little home where I could relax.

I was grateful for the employment as I needed to support myself, and also try to save some money to put towards the rest of my journey. Information was very hard to find, so my search became very slow and often unproductive. I was still on my guard, as the feeling of being followed had not left me. I would try to vary my route when possible. Was this real or of my imagining? I was not quite sure. What on earth had my parents done to warrant all of this intrigue? I decided that when I moved on I would have to undergo a complete change of identity, but that would be for later. For now I was happy to be Swedish Anna working at Macy's department store.

Chapter Twenty Seven

Fun Times

The months passed, I settled into my new employment, and even enjoyed the journey to and from my work. The overhead railway would take me from my home right into Herald Square. I loved sitting and watching as the city rolled out beneath me. Then one day I was called into the office and told I had been promoted to counter work.

In the meanwhile, I had changed out of all recognition. My hair was cut short in a bob, and more shockingly, my skirts had become shorter too. I felt that Aunty K would have approved. I had also made some new friends – Elizabeth, whom we called Lizzie, Mary, William, Robert, and of course Alice. The six of us became a little gang and we would spend our leisure time together when we could. Sundays were our day off, and we would often go to Central Park and walk around the lake, sometimes ride on the carousel or visit the zoo.

On special occasions we would go to Luna on Coney Island. The two boys regularly played tennis and we would later meet up in Evelyn Nesbit's Tea Rooms. I loved our trips out, but I loved my visits to the jazz club even more. These were special treats for when I had enough money.

One evening the gang wanted to go to a new place called Russkiy Medved, where you could eat and listen to balalaika music. It was wonderful. I said nothing of my past to my friends, but sat in the dim light thinking of my life by the lake, and of all the people I had known. So much had happened to my homeland, I felt swamped by sadness. It did not feel right to be enjoying myself in New York. With difficulty, I put my smile back on my face and carried on enjoying the evening. Back in my little home I cried, for the Russia I would never see again, for Aunty K and my joyous time in Romania, for the suffering I had seen, for my parents and for me.

Back at work, everything was as normal. The shop, or as they called it here, the store, was so busy. I loved all the colours, the lights, even the noise, the excited chatter of the shoppers and the ringing of the tills. The store was large, set over several floors, which were linked by beautiful wooden escalators. I was fascinated by them and rode on them whenever I could. I had been moved to the jewellery counter and worked with two older American women, Betty and Emily. We made a good team. I struck up a rapport with the younger male clients, many of whom bought the most beautiful trinkets for their loved ones.

When I could, I would go to the library to search for clues. During my talks with Alice, I learned that the direct route from Gothenburg to New York had only started in 1920, just before I had set sail. Prior to that, the route was much more complex. Travellers would sail to Hull in England, then cross by train to Liverpool, and from there catch a boat to America. I realised that this must have been the way my parents had travelled, if indeed they had come to America.

My sense of purpose was beginning to dim, and my quest seemed less and less important. I had become distracted with all that New York had to offer. My search came back sharply into focus one day when I came across a torn piece of newspaper used as packing in one of the stockroom cases. I stared at the grainy picture looking up at me from the news sheet. It was of a man, I suppose, in his early fifties, with a small dark-haired woman standing by his side. I read the section of print that was left, but kept coming back to the picture.

Their surname was unfamiliar, but there was something in their look that drew me to them. I pocketed the fragment and went back to my work. Later at home I studied the article looking for clues. There was very little except for the year, and half of the name of the paper. It was from two years earlier and was in reference to an award of some kind. At least it was somewhere to start my renewed search.

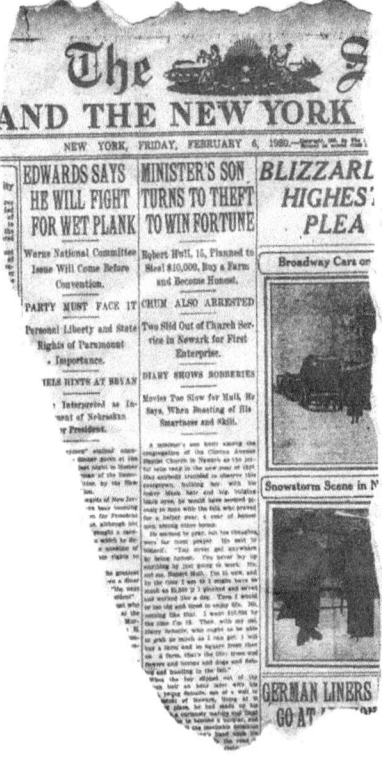

I asked for a half day off, and spent the time in the library. I was directed to the archive section where copies of old newspapers were kept. After some time I found the picture and with it the whole article. The man was a professor of some repute and had come to New York for a ceremony in recognition of his work in engineering. I stared and stared at the picture and I became more and more convinced that I knew these people. It was more a feeling than anything else, after all I had only been 3 years old when my parents had left. I looked particularly at the woman and convinced myself that I could see likenesses of both Aunty A and Aunty K. Could this really be them? I hardly dared to hope. My father had had thick golden hair, but this man had very little. The only other thing I remembered about him was his voice, and his story telling when putting me to bed. It was so difficult to tell.

I would also need to find out how and when this couple arrived in America. I looked for other articles regarding the man and found that they did indeed arrive in America from Liverpool on the White Star Line ship, the *Celtic*, in 1902. It had arrived in August of that year.

The newspaper said that their names were Rybek and Rusalka Sjonsson. I remembered Aunty K telling me of their play names when growing up, father was called the tall fair fisherman (Rybek) and mother the little mermaid (Rusalka). Indeed, all three sisters were all known as the pretty mermaids in the village. Was it just coincidence, or had I finally found some real proof of their existence? The article also said that he was visiting from a university in Massachusetts. Although it was two years before, I felt strongly that they would still be there.

The winter season was upon us and the store was extremely busy. The tills rang out constantly as people prepared for their Christmas celebrations, the animated window displays captivating children and parents alike. The city itself was festooned in lights, and decorated Christmas trees could be seen in the windows of the stores and houses. Our gang liked to go skating in Prospect Park where the boat house area had been recently converted to a skate park, Afterwards, in the cafe there, we would warm up with hot drinks and pastries. I loved the cold, it reminded me of home, my real home. I was determined to go searching again in the spring.

Betty kindly invited me to her home for the Christmas meal, which I gratefully accepted. I wondered what Aunty K and Carl Gustav would be doing, I missed them so much. The rest of the holiday was spent looking forward to New Year's Eve, and going to the Roseland Ballroom with my friends, and later to Times Square to watch the traditional ball drop at midnight.

What a year, I had enjoyed every minute. New York was certainly the most exciting place I had ever lived, and I loved being there. This new year, 1922, was also going to be a good year, I felt it strongly in my heart.

Chapter Twenty Eight

Dilemmas

After the excitement of the holidays, it was business as usual, the store counters being readied for the next main theme, Easter.

By now I was a well-established employee and had become one of the top sales people. I enjoyed the whole atmosphere. The jewellery counter was always busy, and I had built up a good relationship with the regular clients. Having come from a relatively poor background, I was staggered at the wealth of some of the people, but not jealous. My time in Romania with Aunty K had given me riches beyond compare, not in terms of money, but in experiences that money could not buy. The other members of our gang worked on different floors, but we met up when we could. I felt really at home with my friends and life was very good.

I had a great dilemma, what to do next. Should I give up my friends, my employment and my home, to chase what still may be a dream and dead end, or give up on my quest after so many years of searching. I needed to think about things most carefully. I had also become close with William in the past year. He was of English descent, his family having arrived from London the previous century. After some months of walking out together, I decided to take the chance and tell him the truth about myself and my quest.

One Sunday after our walk in Central Park with the rest of the gang, William and I wandered off on our own. I decided to take the opportunity and told him that I needed to talk to him about matters of a serious nature. I assured him that it was only regarding my background. Poor William, he looked so uncomfortable, and I thought in that moment, that we did not know each other well enough, and so decided that it was a bad idea. I apologised and said it would keep for another time. He looked so relieved. I felt disappointed but said nothing. We rejoined the others, but I knew that something had changed between us. We slipped back into our friendship group and life went on as before.

It did, however, have one positive affect. I realised that I would have to finish my quest before I could be totally honest with anyone. And so it was with renewed vigour that I continued my search. The decision to move on was made. New York had been good to me, I enjoyed my job, I loved my little home and I liked being with my friends, but this was not why I had come here. I felt that I had come so far on my quest and desperately needed to know some answers. I did not speak of it to the others.

The couple in the picture were from the engineering section of the Massachusetts Institute of Technology, situated in Boston, so that was where I would start. I would use my few days of holiday to continue my search. I pretended that I was going to Chicago to see Hannah, but instead I travelled north. I had grown very weary of all the subterfuge and longed for a settled life. I had received a letter from Aunty K with all of her news, which also said I could return to them anytime I pleased. My welfare was still in their thoughts, I was deeply touched.

Alice came to the station with me, her intention also to visit relatives. This could be awkward, I thought, but fortunately her train was earlier than mine, and with relief, I waved her off. This was the first time since I had travelled on the train at 15, going to stay with Aunty E, that I had travelled on my own. I was apprehensive. Once settled into my seat, I relaxed and stared out of the window at the countryside rushing by. My head was full of questions. Would my parents recognise me? Would they be pleased to see me? Would their identities still be safe? Was I doing the right thing for us all? Such dilemmas. I looked around the carriage, but no one was paying any heed to me. To lead anyone to my parents after all of this time would be a tragedy.

The city came into view and I got ready to disembark. I needed to find a small hotel for my stay. I had decided on a hotel as I thought it more anonymous than a boarding house. However, I looked at the advertisements around the station and realised that a hotel would be too expensive. I opted for a boarding house that was near to South Station, where I was now standing.

I found the street and was relieved to find that it was a rather pleasant place. Inside was a homely atmosphere.

I booked in and after a short rest went for a walk around the local area. At a small cabin I bought a newspaper and asked the vendor if he knew the location of the Institute. He did, of course, and was able to give me directions. As it was already late afternoon, I decided to go the next day, and so made my way back to my lodgings.

An evening meal was provided, of which I gladly partook. I sat in the cosy dining room with the other visitors. We were an odd assortment, some were travelling salesmen from many different places, at least according to their accents. There was a young couple with a small child sitting with two older people, grandparents I supposed, then there was me. I was quite the object of attention, so I smiled sweetly and sat at one of the empty tables. Within minutes I was joined by two elderly ladies. Naturally, they wanted to know my business, so I made up a story about visiting my brother who was studying for a doctorate at the university. This seemed to suffice.

The following day, after a reasonably restful night, I would start my search in earnest. The best place for information, I reasoned, would be the library. I learned that the campus had been moved to a new place, at Cambridge, which thankfully was not too far away if I travelled by subway, which had been built especially to join both places. I had been on the subway in New York a few times, so it was not too daunting.

I arrived in Cambridge and went straight to the main building of the Institute, a beautiful brick building built in the colonial style of the day. In fact there were many beautiful buildings in both Boston and Cambridge. I took my crumpled newspaper clipping and showed it to the very serious-looking woman in the Records Department. She wanted to know why I was searching, so I told her it was on behalf of my father's brother, to pass on news of a family illness. She studied the article, then me, and then proceeded to look through a large filing cabinet, one of many in the room. Finally, she said that the man I wanted was in the Department for Chemical Engineering. My heart thudded in my chest and I tried very hard to keep my emotions under control.

With her directions etched deeply into my memory, I set off to locate the place, and whoever I would find there. I steeled myself for disappointment. I walked around the campus until I saw the building, and stood outside gathering my thoughts and my nerve, before stepping through the door to meet my destiny.

Chapter Twenty Nine

Resolutions

I was shown to a side office and asked to wait. My heartbeat drummed loudly in my ears. A shadow appeared in the doorway window. I stood rigidly to attention and held my breath. The door opened and in stepped a woman. A small dark-haired woman, with grey at her temples, who looked me up and down. I introduced myself as Anna Neilsson, I was still unsure of saying too much, as I did not really know to whom I was speaking.

She in turn introduced herself as Frida Sjonsson. This was the surname that I had read in the newspaper, not her travelling name of Russalka. Was there some recognition? It was hard to be sure, she was very guarded. I said hello and put my animal charm bracelet down on the table. Her expression did not alter as she said that the professor was not available, but she would set up a meeting for 11 o'clock the next day. Surprisingly, she did not ask me the purpose of my visit.

I picked up my bracelet and left. It was a very strange encounter and I did not know what to think, it was not at all how I had imagined it to be. Still, at least it was a meeting and I had not been completely dismissed. Back in my lodgings I studied the little bracelet, it no longer fitted my adult wrist, but I carried it with me everywhere I went. After my evening meal, I stayed in my room to reflect on what had happened so far and what may occur the next day. I slept badly, worrying that this may be another dead end and I would have to start my search anew. I awoke feeling tense and tired. I ate little breakfast then slowly made my way back to the Institute.

Again I was shown into the austere office where I waited, pacing around the room. I heard footsteps in the corridor, then the door opened and in stepped the woman followed by a tall fair man. The people from my newspaper article. We all sat down and after the hellos he asked me where I had obtained the bracelet. I told him that an aunt had given it to me when I was a child. It was a very stilted conversation and he was obviously very guarded, I could have been sent from any authority to find them. I told them some information about Aunty A and my upbringing by the lake.

A few awkward minutes passed, so I pressed boldly on. I told them of life with the fishermen, my move to the capital to live with Aunty E, and of my happy time in Romania with Aunty K. I also told them of my time as a Red Cross nurse, of crossing into Sweden, and my eventual arrival in New York. I gave them an outline of my life. They listened intently but said nothing. It was disconcerting, but I realised that a good spy could have learnt this information. I understood their reticence. Finally, I said I had one more piece of information and it involved the strange nature of my real name and birth date, and how I had used them in my search.

There was a prolonged silence in the room and the woman started to cry softly. The man looked into my blue eyes, which mirrored his own, and as recognition dawned, we three stood in that bare office and embraced each other. A dam burst in me and I sobbed as never before. I had waited so long for this moment and even though I had seen it in my head, I was not ready for the reality of it.

It was decided that we should meet up in a small local park where we could talk with less chance of being overheard as long as we were vigilant. They still had not told me anything of themselves, their years of hiding their identities still very strong in their behaviour. I was happy to go anywhere as I was eager to learn about their lives, and in a small corner of my mind I wanted to know how they could have left me behind.

The professor had lectures for the next few hours and we would meet up with him later. The woman, I knew, was my mother. I felt it most strongly, and had really known from the moment I saw the newspaper cutting. The man I was less sure of, although there was something comforting in his voice. We left the campus and walked to a small cafe in the park where we waited for the professor.

There were very few people about, so we spoke in hushed tones. She told me how she had wept inconsolably at having to leave me, but felt it was the safest thing to do for all of us. They were not sure of their survival but leaving me behind would ensure mine. They had travelled through Russia to Murmansk and from there by boat to Sweden. Like Aunty K and I, they had found work where they could, becoming Swedish in the process. The journey up through Russia explained why I had no real sense of them while travelling with Aunty K. They too had eventually left from Gothenburg, arriving in America via Liverpool. I explained that the war had played a great part in my life, the images of which would never be completely erased, and was the reason for the search having taken so long.

The professor joined us, but he was still very wary. I did not know what more I could do to convince him, I had shown him the bracelet. Then I thought about the locket that Aunty K had given me. I showed it to him, and he very obviously recognised it. It had been his mother's, he remembered her wearing it and also that she had given it to Aunty E on her 18th birthday. It brought to mind a conversation between Aunty E and Aunty K about something they had given to me on my 18th birthday. I had always thought the locket belonged to my mother's family, but actually it was from my father's line. Finally, he believed that I was indeed his daughter.

We spent the rest of the day reminiscing about the lake and life there before fate intervened. I told them about Aunty A and Aunty F, but mostly about my beloved Aunty K. I told them of the death of Stephan and how after many years she had again found love with Carl Gustav. They were surprised at the marriage of Aunty E. There was so much to talk about but so little time. I had to go back to New York that evening as I still had my work in the store. My mother said she would try to visit me so we could get to know each other again. Father would stay up in Cambridge, but assured me we would meet up when possible.

I sadly took my leave of them both and made my way back to the boarding house. When the bill was paid I went to the station. I had many mixed emotions as I later climbed into my bed in my little New York haven.

Chapter Thirty

What Is, Is. What Cannot Be, Cannot Be.

The next few weeks passed quickly. I was busy at my work and fell back into the way of life in the store and spending Sundays with the gang. My mother came to see me once a month, and we would meet, as if by accident, in Central Park. I told my friends that she was a relative of Carl Gustav. My father never came, at least not to New York. I still had no real answers and my curiosity grew and grew. My mother would tell me of their early life in the village, of their journeys and how they had come to America. It was all very measured, and I wondered when the adventurous, beautiful young woman I had heard about had disappeared. Years of hiding had taken its toll. I suppose I expected it to be a glamorous, exciting life and for her to be like Aunty K, who I missed very much.

It was very hard for her to mend our bond, I had been 3 years old when she last saw me. Now she was faced with a determined young woman who had lived through the turn of the century, the war, and the dawn of a new age. However, we made the best relationship that we could. I loved her, but I could not shake off the feeling of guilt that I loved the idea of her more than the reality.

I was desperate to speak with my father and ask him all of the questions that had driven my quest for the last 10 years. On one of my secret visits to see him in Cambridge I decided to be brave and question him. To my surprise, he was happy to talk. I asked him to tell me the story of his life. He smiled, took a deep breath, and began.

He had, as I knew, met my mother when he was 20 and they had fallen in love. They married, and he continued his work at the factory. After a year, I was born, and he was moved to the research section. There he found plans for devices that would ultimately harm mankind and it did not fit with his ethos of life. He realised that there would be a profound and devastating effect on populations if the technology were ever to be used by the military. He decided he had to act, to destroy the blueprints, all research papers and formulas.

It had affected him deeply and became a very fraught time for him and my mother. They decided they had to leave. I was almost 3 years old, so the decision was made to leave me with my aunt, for their sake and for mine. Aunty A moved to another lakeside village, passing me off as her daughter. My birth name was Anastasia. Their intention had always been to go to America. There had been much talk of this place at the factory, but he had kept his interest in emigration a close secret. He played the good patriot until the day he left.

They had become fugitives once his sabotage was discovered, and finally after two years they had reached America. They had an arduous journey on the *SS Rollo* to Hull in England, then across the country by rail to the port of Liverpool where they boarded the *SS Celtic*. Not for them the easy trip that I had, but of course it had been 1902 when they travelled to America. After clearance at Ellis Island, they travelled via New York to Boston, the location of the Institute. A new country and new names. Mother worked as a seamstress, while Father had enrolled as a student in the engineering section, supplementing their income by working at the newspaper office as a runner. Through years of hard study he had worked his way up to the position of professor.

I listened patiently as he talked on, some of the pieces finally falling into place. I had been born on a cold December night, over the midnight hour of New Year's Eve into the year 1896. When they fled they decided to leave me behind, both for my safety and their own. He said nothing of the strange numbers on the back of the portrait painting. He had insisted that I be known as Algebra, translated from the Arabic as "reunion of broken parts". A wish for the future.

The documents he had destroyed were for the manufacture and use of chemical weapons in the time of war, in the controlling of crowds, and ultimately in ending life. His heart and head would not allow for that, and so, with his plans carried out, they had left.

As I was already a curious child, he knew that I would look for them. I had, on reflection, had so much help from the aunties, of whom I now had even greater respect. I finally understood why the authorities would want to find them. They had committed an act of treason and set research back decades.

I really wanted to know about the numbers on the back of the painting. He smiled and said that I had instinctively known what they meant, otherwise I would not be there.

My head was reeling, and I felt quite faint, I was so conflicted. Part of me was proud of him for taking a stand against potential oppression, but the other part was hurt and angry at being left behind. It was overwhelming and I felt a strong need to be back at my little flat in New York.

Once home in my safe place, over the next months I learned to relax and enjoy the company of my parents, only time would tell if it had all been worthwhile. For the first time I started to like my strange name, and I also worked out the mystery.

The numbers were the coordinates for New York, their original destination when fleeing from persecution, and the other half was a message for me, from Boole's Second Law of Thought:

"the given probabilities of any system of events, to determine the consequent probability of any other event, which is logically connected to those events"

They knew I would come, and I knew deep down that I would find them.

One evening there was a knock on my door, and there stood the strange man from the ship. He held up a badge and in a commanding tone he said, "Miss Neilsson, I must ask you to accompany me…"

List of Characters

Algebra / Anna Neilsson
Parents – Natasha and Sergei
Aunty A – Aninya
Aunty E – Elena
Mikhail – professor / Aunty E's husband

Aunty K – Ekaterina, known as Katya
Uncle Stephan – Aunty K's husband

Tomas and Lukas – fishermen
Petyr, Olga, Katerina and parents – Moscow train
Svetlana, Nicki and Alex – train
Brasov Shipping Office:
Natalya
Yana
Hans
Mrs Leminski
Two officials
Small shabby man
Maria – friend of Aunty K

Atila and Bebe – blacksmiths, Romania
Margarite – mother of Atila and Bebe

Hercules – cart horse
Gypsy camp – musicians and dancers

Valentina – gypsy camp

Alexander and Christobel – university friends of Mikhail

Parents of Alexander

Old folk – parents of doctor
Agnis – worker on the farm
Erik – son of Agnis

Elsa Brandstrom – Swedish nurse
Livy and Riina – Finnish nurses (on troop train)
Doctors – at the Helsinki camp

Army officers

Sven, Anna, Niclaus, Christina, Freya, Olga and Frederik – Swedish farm family
Baikal – horse
Russian soldiers – hospital train
German soldiers – POW exchange train

Various unnamed travellers

Carl Gustav – rich Swedish gentleman

American-Swedish Shipping Line – Gothenburg

Sinister man on *SS Drottningholm*

Hannah's American family – Chicago

Lizzie, Florence, Mary, Alice, William and Robert – New York friends

Betty and Emily – co-workers at Macy's department store

Librarian

Boarding house occupants – Boston

Records clerk

Rybek and Russalka Sjonsson

Locations

Russia
Lake Baikal
Irkutsk
Moscow
St Petersburg

Romania
Brasov
Sighișoara
Suceava

Moldova
Odesa

Finland
Helsinki
Tornio

Sweden
Harpandra
Karlstad
Vänersborg
Gothenburg

USA
Ellis Island

Chicago
New York
Boston
Cambridge

Acknowledgements

My thanks to Simon Hadfield and Penny Knight for their support in everything.

To Lez Harvey for the cover design, horse photograph and information on horse behaviour.

To Chris Hadfield and Steph Summers for the ageing and reworking of my own photographs into the illustrations format.

'Troops and Nurses' photograph and 'Poster and Newspaper fragment' photograph – historic, non-copyright.

To Christine Emery and Linda Boisson for their proofreading and critiques.

To Adrienne Allinson and Karen Crick for patiently listening to my ramblings on every phone call.

To my colleagues at work, the two Joannes who endured endless updates on the story and who did not complain once, at least not in my presence.

To Tamsin, Máire, Becky, Tanis and all staff at Grosvenor House Publishing Ltd. for their support, advice and encouragement.

And to my three cats, Ellie-May, Mali-Blue and Devon Lacey who put up with my frustrations, my highs and my lows during the creation of this story.

Research:

To Wikipedia and the many sites for background information on Russia in World War One, the early Red Cross, and the railways at the turn of the 20th century.

Information on New York in the early 1920s.

Own visits to the various cities.

Photographic archives of various cities and towns from 1900 to 1920: For the checking of details of buildings, fashion and transport of the time: Moscow, Brasov, St Petersburg, Odesa, Helsinki, Karlstad, Vänersborg, Gothenburg, New York and Boston.

History of Elsa Brandstrom – Swedish nurse

White Star Shipping Line ships 1902

Swedish American Line ships 1920

History of POW exchanges in World War One between Finland and Sweden.